THE LOST MOTHERS' CLUB

The Kidnapping

Ann Westmoreland

AuthorHouse™
1663 Liberty Drive
Bloomington, IN 47403
www.authorhouse.com
Phone: 1 (800) 839-8640

Published by AuthorHouse 06/03/2015

ISBN: 978-1-5049-1441-3 (sc)
ISBN: 978-1-5049-1455-0 (e)

Library of Congress Control Number: 2015908513

Print information available on the last page.

Any people depicted in stock imagery provided by Thinkstock are models, and such images are being used for illustrative purposes only. Certain stock imagery © Thinkstock.

This book is printed on acid-free paper.

This book is dedicated to my wonderful husband, Marvin, my four wonderful children, Cheri (who was taken from us too soon), Suzanne, Lisa, and Glynn and my six wonderful grandchildren, David, Jackie, Mark, Rebecca, Elizabeth, and Mary without whom life would have no meaning.

Prologue

All over the world there are young girls who do not have a mother for one reason or another. Some of these daughters have lost their mothers through death, but a great many of them have lost their mothers through indifference, ignorance, or illness, both mental and physical. Also, some mothers are not able to keep their babies when they are born, even though they love them dearly. A loving family usually adopts these babies.

Motherless girls all have one thing in common:

they miss their moms throughout their lives. When deprived of their mother at a young age, for whatever reason, they all feel the longing for a close relationship with the mother who carried them for nine months. They envy those close to them who have the benefit of mothers who care.

Most motherless girls become very strong willed and do things most girls wouldn't think to do. They set their mind to do something, and they do it, regardless of what other people think or do. They become doers in their community, usually concentrating on the poor or weak. Many become health care workers, teachers, counselors, or other related fields. These girls give much of themselves to others throughout their lives.

Chapter One

Jenny sat cross-legged on the floor of her room facing a Monopoly board. Mandy, her new friend, sat on the opposite side of the board with the Monopoly bank money into neat piles beside her. Jenny frowned as she asked, "Did you hear about Molly's mom?"

"No. What happened?" Mandy asked.

"Well, she left Molly and her dad."

"Left? Why?" Mandy's eyes grew wide. "Where did she go?"

"I heard Argo and my dad talking when Dad came home from work. Calvin's mom heard that she has a boyfriend and left Mandy and her dad last Saturday."

"Maybe," Mandy said, "that's why Molly looked like she'd been crying in school today. I tried to talk to her, but she just walked away."

"I can't understand how anyone can leave their family like that," Jenny said. "My mother left because she died, not because she had a boyfriend. I don't know how I'd feel if she just walked out on us."

"I'd feel terrible," Mandy confided. "It's hard enough for me since my mom's been in the hospital. It wasn't her choice to get sick and have to live there for a while."

"I didn't know your mom was in the hospital," Jenny said. "What's wrong with her?"

"My dad won't talk about it much, but it has something to do with her brain. It doesn't work right all the time. She does some strange things and says strange things."

Jenny was intrigued. "What kind of things?"

"Oh, she says she hears voices, and they tell her what to do."

"That's weird," Jenny said. "How long does she have to stay there?"

"Until she gets better. At least that's what my dad said." Mandy changed the subject, for she was starting to get tears in her eyes just thinking about her mother. "I didn't know your mom died. What happened?"

Jenny looked sad. "She died in a car accident. A drunk driver hit her."

Mandy looked horrified. She put her hands over her mouth. "That's terrible! How old were you?"

"I was three." A single tear slid down Jenny's cheek. She wiped it away with the back of her hand.

"You know, there are a lot of us who only have one parent," Mandy said. "Angie's mom just doesn't want her."

"Doesn't want her! What do you mean?"

"Well, she said that her mom dropped her off at her grandmother's house when she was little and just left."

"Just left her?" Jenny asked. "Just like that? That's unbelievable!"

"Just like that. She sees her sometimes at Christmas and sometimes in the summer, if her mom feels like it. She didn't even get a birthday card or a Christmas present from her last year. And the summer before that, she asked Angie to come to see her, but all her mom did was hang out with her new boyfriend and leave Angie in her apartment alone."

"That's terrible!" Jenny said. "I didn't know that she lived with her grandmother."

"She doesn't now," Mandy explained. "Her

grandmother was very sick and had to go into the hospital for an operation, so she called Angie's dad to come and get her. She's been living with him ever since."

"Why didn't her dad have her before that?" Jenny asked.

"I don't know. Angie didn't tell me that."

"Susan doesn't have a mom, either," Jenny said.

"She doesn't?" Mandy asked. "I didn't know that. What happened to her mom?"

"Her mom had a bad heart. She needed surgery, but she died before it could be done."

Mandy looked sad. "I thought I was the only one living without my mother. I didn't know who to talk to about it, because I was afraid no one would understand."

"You know what?" Jenny asked. "We should start a club."

"What kind of club?"

"One for girls like us, girls with no mothers."

"I have a mother," Mandy said.

"I mean for girls who are not living with their mothers."

"Oh. You mean a club where we could go to talk. I'd like that. Sometimes I feel so lonely and need someone to talk to. My dad is no help there. He's tired when he comes home from work, then he has to cook, do the washing, and all the other things my mom did before she went to the hospital. Besides that, he doesn't like to talk about my mother."

"I'm lucky, I guess," Jenny said. "I have Argo. She's our nanny. She came to live with us when I was little and has been there for my sister and me ever since. We can talk to her about anything."

"Let's make a list," Mandy suggested, "of all the girls we know without moms living with them. Then we can ask them if they want to be in a club."

"Good idea," Jenny said. She jumped up and ran to her desk. She opened the top drawer and took out a small notebook and a pencil. The Monopoly game was forgotten, even though Jenny had been winning. This was much more important. Jenny chewed on the eraser end of the pencil and tightened her eyebrows in concentration. "Okay, we have you," she put one finger up, "me, Molly, Angie, and Susan." She counted off the last four with the rest of her fingers. "That's five."

"What about Christy?" Mandy asked. "Her mom's in jail."

"In jail!" Jenny exclaimed. "No way! Why?"

"My dad saw it in the newspaper" Mandy explained. "She got busted for drugs."

"That's awful," Jenny said. "Who's taking care of her?"

"She moved in with her aunt and uncle. They live close, so she didn't have to change schools."

"What about her father?" Jenny asked.

"Oh, Christy's mom and dad got a divorce last

year, and he's living in Arizona or somewhere near there with his new wife," Mandy explained.

"Jail moms work for me," Jenny said. "As long as we're adding names, what about Jackie? Her mom's in the army. Her dad's taking care of her while her mom is stationed in Turkey for six months."

"That works for me," Mandy said. "How many is that?"

"Well, we had five, and Christy and Jackie make seven. Let's ask them if they want to be in a club at school tomorrow," Jenny said. "We can probably meet here. We have a rec room in the basement, and Argo will probably fix snacks for us."

"Argo would do that? She wouldn't care?" Mandy asked. Her mom, even when she was well and lived at home, always wanted Mandy to come home alone. Her mother never let her bring her friends home. Mandy's friends were always too noisy, too messy, or they gave her mom a headache.

"Naw. Argo's cool. She likes me to have my friends here. She says it's so she can get to know them, so she knows if they're people I should hang out with."

"Wow!" Mandy exclaimed. "She must really care." Mandy was slightly jealous, for no one seemed to care that much about her. "And she's not even your real mother," she added, still not really believing. "No wonder you don't look like the rest of us."

"What do you mean?" Jenny didn't understand. Ever since Argo had lived with her family, she had treated her and Marylou like they were her own children. Jenny had just assumed that her friends' mothers and stepmothers all treated their kids like Argo treated her, with care and respect.

"I mean," Mandy said, "that Angie and Susan both look like they care for themselves. Lots of times they come to school with dirty hair or messy clothes, never clean and neat like you always are. You don't look like someone without a mom."

"I get dirty," Jenny said, "especially when I go fishing with Calvin." Calvin lived next door to

Jenny and had been her best friend since she moved in a couple of years ago.

"That's different. That's new dirt, not old dirt."

Jenny looked confused. "I don't understand."

"New dirt," Mandy explained, "is fun dirt, dirt that you get into when you're playing. Old dirt is when you don't wash your hair for three or four days or when you wear the same clothes more than one day in a row without washing them. Old dirt is when no one cares enough about you to see that your hair is combed or your hands are washed before you eat."

Jenny did understand. Her friend, Pete, lived in old dirt for a long time while his father traveled, and his step-mom made him live in the basement while his dad was away.

She suddenly felt lucky to have Argo, even though it was a pain to have to take a bath every night, sometimes during a really good TV program, and it was annoying to wait to go out to play until Argo combed her hair and put it into a neat ponytail.

Jenny and Marylou complained to Argo about these things, but she would just hug them and tell them to be patient. She always insisted, too, that everything they wore each day had to be put in the hamper to be washed. They never were allowed to wear the same thing two days in a row.

"Christy never looks dirty," Jenny said.

"That's probably because Christy's aunt probably treats her just like her own kids, making her take showers, wash her hair and change her clothes," Mandy explained.

"Oh," Jenny said looking thoughtful. "Let's put the game away and go talk to Argo about meeting here."

"OK," Mandy answered. She picked up the Monopoly money and stored it neatly in the box. She was glad she had moved in across the street from such a good friend, one who cared enough to listen to her. It had been hard moving from a big house to a small house and leaving her other friends, but her dad had explained that the hospital was very expensive, and they couldn't afford the big house anymore. He sold some of the furniture, but he let Mandy keep everything that was hers, for which she was grateful. She still had all her stuffed animals and dolls to talk to when her father was too busy to listen to her. Now, she had a friend, a friend who understood her problem, a friend who listened to her and was interested in the things she had to say.

Chapter Two

Jenny walked around her bedroom holding the cordless phone. She had called Mandy to see if she had talked to Christy and Jackie about the club, which they simply decided to name The Lost Mothers' Club. Jenny talked to Molly and Angie. Molly said she'd call Susan when she got home, after her dance lesson. Her grandmother picked her up from school and took her to her lesson, now that her mother was gone.

"Molly cried when I told her about the club,"

Jenny said into the phone. "She'd been worried that no one would want to hang with her after her mom left."

"Why would she think that?" Mandy asked.

"I don't really know," Jenny said. "We like her for herself, not because of her mom."

"Does she live in that big house on the next corner, with the swimming pool?"

"That's the one," Jenny said. "Isn't it awesome?"

"Why would her mom want to leave such a mansion?"

"Beats me," Jenny said. She shrugged, even though Mandy wasn't there to see it. "I went swimming there once last summer. A butler answered the door, a cook brought us lunch, and a maid cleaned up."

"Wow!" Mandy exclaimed. "They must be really rich."

"Molly doesn't act like she has a lot of money,"

Jenny said. "She's not a snob, and she doesn't talk about all the things she has. She just acts like just another kid."

"I wouldn't have known she was rich, if Calvin hadn't pointed out her house when we rode to the store on our bikes. You're right. She's really sweet, and she doesn't act like a spoiled rich kid."

"Did you talk to Christy and Jackie?" Jenny asked.

"I talked to Jackie, but Christy had to go to the dentist right after school. Jackie was going to talk to her tonight."

"Molly and Angie said they'd like to come to our club, as long as we didn't ask a lot of questions," Jenny said. "I told them that they could come, but we were only getting together because we were all without mothers, and that we wouldn't ask them any questions. They could tell us as much or as little as they wanted, and that we just wanted to be friends, to be there if they needed us, or if we needed them."

"That's cool," Mandy said. "Jackie was definitely interested. She thought she was the only one who had to deal with such a problem. She really misses her mom, since she left for Turkey with the army."

"This was definitely one of our better ideas," Jenny said. "I'm so glad we thought of it." Jenny heard Argo call up the stairs for her to come to dinner. "I've got to eat. I'll talk to you tomorrow at school."

"Okay," Mandy said. "This is going to be fun. I've never been in a club before."

"Neither have I," Jenny admitted. "I really don't know what to do in a club."

"Maybe we could just hang out and be friends with the others," Mandy said.

"Sounds good," Jenny replied. "I've got to go. Bye."

At the dinner table, Jenny asked her dad and Argo what people did in a club. Mr. Jenkins said that people join clubs because they have a common interest, such as golf or tennis. Then they get together and play the game. Argo said that some clubs are formed because people have the same feelings or ideas, and they get together to discuss them and go to places they all like, just as an art club would go to an art museum. Neither of these explanations helped Jenny very much, except the getting together part. Maybe they could meet and play a game or rent a movie and watch it together. The important thing, she decided, was just getting together, to be there for each other, to be able to talk to someone else who doesn't have a mother living with them. Jenny had tried to talk to her sister about it, but Marylou didn't want to talk to her about anything. She had felt alone in her problem for a long time. She loved Argo, but it wasn't the same. She missed her mom. She felt that the other girls in the club would feel the same way.

"What can we do when we get together for the first time?" Jenny asked Argo while they were clearing the table. "Well, you could make some cookies. That's always fun," Argo answered. "I can pick up the ingredients at the supermarket tomorrow."

"Cool! Argo, you're the greatest!" Jenny put the dishes on the counter and hugged her nanny. "Can we make chocolate chip cookies?"

"I don't know why not. I'll look up the recipe and leave it out for you. I'll be out on the back porch on Saturday, if you girls need to ask any questions."

"Thanks." Jenny knew she was lucky to have Argo. If she couldn't have her mom, Argo was the next best thing, better than some of her friends' real moms.

* * * * * * * * *

That night, Jenny had trouble getting to sleep. Her mind was filled with thoughts of the club, thoughts that spun around the fact that so many of her friends were without one parent or the other. She had only two friends, Jamie and Terri, who lived with both their mother and father. Calvin, her friend next door, lived with just his mother. His dad left Calvin and his mom just before Jenny moved in. Josh and Jeremy, two more friends from school, were cousins. Both their moms left when they were little, and their dads, who were brothers, moved in together to raise the boys.

Jenny wanted The Lost Mothers' Club to work. She wanted the girls to become good friends, friends who would be there for each other forever. Argo still met with her old high school girlfriends. Once a month, they would go somewhere together, usually out to eat. Those nights, Jenny, Marylou, and their dad either had pizza delivered or grilled hamburgers in the back yard.

Jenny worried about what the club members would do, if they would all get along, even though they had a common bond. She worried that Calvin would feel left out. After all, they had been best friends for more than two years. She worried that Marylou would make fun of them and cause trouble during the meetings if they met at her house. Jenny tossed and turned, finally falling asleep around eleven-thirty.

At school the next day, Jenny yawned through math, and couldn't concentrate on the story the class was reading in literature. Mandy passed her a note in social studies about Susan wanting to join the club. Molly had talked to her that morning.

After school, Jenny walked home with Calvin and told him about the club. She hoped he wouldn't be too upset, but Calvin pleasantly surprised her.

"The club sounds awesome, Jenny," Calvin said. "I think it's a good idea. Maybe Josh and Jeremy would like to start a club with me."

"We can still be friends," Jenny said.

"Absolutely," Calvin answered. "We can still go fishing, play in my tree house, and hang out when the club doesn't meet." They both knew then that their friendship was not in trouble, that their relationship was strong, strong enough to last for a long, long time.

"I'm glad you're not mad," Jenny said.

"Why would I be mad?" Calvin asked.

"Oh, I don't know," Jenny said. "I was worried about that when I went to bed last night."

Calvin stopped walking and faced Jenny. "Well, worry no more. I'm not mad. I'm not upset. You're my best friend. Nothing will change that."

"We have had some good times together, haven't we?" Jenny smiled, thinking of the time Calvin's dog was up in the oak tree in her front yard.

"The best," Calvin grinned. "By the way, Mom's cooking spaghetti tonight. Do you want to come over for supper?"

"I'll have to ask Argo, but I'm sure she won't mind. Come on, I'll race you home!" She broke into a run before Calvin could react. Her long, brown ponytail sailed out behind her like a windsock.

Calvin smiled at his friend and ran to catch up. His backpack bounced on his back with each step. He knew he was fast, but maybe not as fast as Jenny. That didn't matter. What did matter was that they were running together, and together is the way friends should be.

Chapter Three

Saturday morning dawned sunny and bright. Jenny smelled bacon cooking. She hopped out of bed, put on her cat slippers, and ran down the stairs, jumping the last three to land with a thump.

"Mercy!" Argo exclaimed from the kitchen. "It's a wonder you don't fall when you do that."

"I always do that, Argo," Jenny laughed.

"I know you do, but it worries me just the same."

Jenny smiled. She knew that Argo cared. She padded into the kitchen, sniffing delightedly at the biscuit and bacon smells that mingled together. Her mouth watered.

"Today's the big day," Argo said. "What time is your club coming over?"

"Around two o'clock," Jenny answered. "Mandy's going to visit her mom in the hospital this morning, so we decided to meet this afternoon."

"Your cookie ingredients are here on the countertop, except for the butter and eggs. I'll put them out after lunch."

"Thanks, Argo. You're awesome."

"You're welcome, honey. Just be sure to clean up after yourselves."

"We will." Jenny smiled as she buttered a hot biscuit. She stuffed half the biscuit into her mouth then wiped her mouth with the back of her hand.

"Jenny!" Argo exclaimed. "Use a napkin."

"Yes, ma-am," Jenny answered as she grabbed a napkin from the middle of the table. "Where's Dad?"

"He went to Home Mart to get a new lock for the front door," Argo answered.

"Why? What's wrong with the old one?"

"It's hard to lock. He was afraid for us to be here alone with a faulty lock."

"Oh, that's cool." Jenny really didn't see the need for a lock at all, since nothing ever happened in this neighborhood. She always felt safe.

* * * * * * * *

The first three meetings of The Lost Mothers' Club were a success. The girls talked to each other and became closer with each meeting. The cookie making was fun, even though Mandy spilled flour all over the floor. Everyone stopped doing what they were doing to help her clean it up. For the second meeting, Jenny's dad rented a video, and the girls watched it in the rec room in Jenny's basement. The third meeting was a sleep over. Molly said that they could come to her house. Her dad was cool about it and stayed in his den or his bedroom, giving the girls the run of the big house. The cook brought in fancy little sandwiches, chips, and sodas for them to snack on while the girls experimented with the abundant amount of make-up that Molly's mom had left behind, painted their fingernails and toenails, and fixed each others' hair. Then they watched movie channels in Molly's huge bedroom until they fell asleep. In the morning, the cook spread out a buffet breakfast in the dining room from which the girls served themselves. Several of the girls thought they were in Heaven. After swimming in the heated pool, the girls were driven home in Molly's dad's limousine.

* * * * ** *

The fourth meeting was to take place on the Saturday after the sleep over. The girls had planned to go to the mall and see a movie in the theatre, but their plans changed.

That Friday morning, at school, Mandy ran up

to Jenny. "Did you see the police cars last night?" she asked breathlessly.

"I heard them. Why?" Jenny asked.

"My dad took me to the store to get some shampoo, and there were five police cars in front of Molly's house, all with their lights flashing."

"Oh, no!" Jenny gasped. She put her hand over her mouth. "What happened?"

"I don't know," Mandy told her. "I'd ask Molly, but she's not at school."

"I wonder if they were robbed," Jenny said. "They have all those big paintings and stuff."

"If they were just robbed, why didn't Molly come to school?" Mandy asked.

"You're right," Jenny answered. "There's got to be something else. I wonder what it is."

At that moment, Jackie ran up the hallway. Jenny and Mandy had to wait for her to catch her breath before she could gasp out, "Did you hear about Molly?"

"What happened?" Jenny and Mandy asked together.

"She's been kidnapped!" Jackie almost yelled. "You know Molly's maid Sonya? Well, she sings in the choir with my mom in church. Sonya called my mom and told her late last night, because she knew I was friends with Molly."

"That's awful," Jenny said, shock in her voice. "What can we do?"

"What do you mean, what can we do?" Mandy asked. "She's been kidnapped. We're just kids. We can't do anything."

"I'm not so sure about that," Jenny said with confidence in her voice. She tapped her cheek with her finger. "Talk to everyone in the club and tell them to come to my house after school. We'll think of something. After all, we're all girls without mothers to do things for us. We've all had to learn to think for ourselves out of necessity." Jenny clicked her fingers together with a snap. "I know we can help in some way."

* * * * * * * *

At Jenny's house that afternoon, Argo told Jenny and her friends that the news had run stories all day about the kidnapping. She said, "The butler saw two men shove Molly into a white van with ice cream decals all over it. He thought Molly went out to buy ice cream, but the men grabbed her instead. The butler said that Molly fought like a wildcat, kicking one man in the shins, scratching the other man's arm, and stomping on the first man's toe. The whole time she was screaming, 'Let me go! Let me go!' He ran to help her, but while they were shoving her in the van, a woman, who was in the driver's seat, stepped on the gas and peeled off down the street. One man slammed the door while the van was careening off. The whole time, Molly was screaming at the top of her lungs."

"How awful," Jackie said. A tear slid down her cheek. "Why would anyone want to take Molly?"

"For ransom," Argo answered. "The news said that the men sent a ransom note demanding two million dollars by noon on Monday, or they'd kill Molly."

The girls all gasped. Jenny and Mandy put their hands on their chests. Jackie and Susan cried. Christy and Angie hugged each other.

"They already sent a ransom note?" Jenny asked.

"Yes," Argo answered. "It was put in the mailbox of the bank that Molly's dad uses, sometime in the middle of the night. The kidnappers were probably afraid to go to Molly's house because of the police."

"Did they show the note on TV?" Jackie asked.

"No, the police have it," Argo said. "They're probably dusting it for fingerprints. But the news reporter said that the note was made up of cut-out words from a newspaper, glued to a piece of copy paper."

The doorbell rang. Jenny ran to the door and

saw Calvin standing on the front porch. "Come on in, Calvin. We're talking about Molly."

"I thought so," he replied. "I came over to see if I could help."

"Sure, the more the merrier," Jenny said as she pushed the hook up on the screen door. "Argo's been listening to the news all day and found out that the kidnappers want two million dollars by Monday, or they'll kill Molly."

"Yeah, my mom told me," Calvin replied soberly. "I'm glad I'm not rich. I wouldn't want to be kidnapped."

"Yeah, me, too," Jenny answered. She walked back to the living room with Calvin. The girls filled him in on what Argo had told them.

"I know that van!" Calvin shouted. "I've seen it before."

"Where?" Argo asked. "This could be important."

"Out by my dad's new house. I was in the front shooting baskets, when I saw that van drive by."

"That doesn't necessarily mean that the owner lives out there," Argo said. "It could have just been driving by." She rose from the chair and announced that she had to start dinner. "I'm fixing a big lasagna and garlic bread, if any of you girls want to stay. That goes for you, too, Calvin."

"Is she always like that?" Angie asked. Her real mom never asked her friends to dinner; she didn't even want Angie around. And this was just Jenny's nanny.

"Like what?" Jenny asked.

"Nice like that."

"Yeah." Jenny smiled. She knew she was lucky.

* * * * * * * * *

The girls all called their homes and asked to stay for dinner. Calvin ran next door and asked his mom. They all pitched in to help. Most of them had to help at home, so they were used to it. Argo loved having all this help. She just loved being around children.

After the table was cleared and the dishes were put into the dishwasher, The Lost Mothers' Club and Calvin retreated to the basement to plan.

"Just because Argo doesn't think the van is from around my dad's house, doesn't mean that it's not," Calvin said.

"You're right," Jenny said. "That's our first clue to where Molly is being held."

"Is there anyplace around your dad's that she could've been taken?" Angie asked.

"Is there and old farm, or something, out there?" Mandy asked.

"How many times did you see the van?" Susan asked.

"Wait," Calvin protested. He put both of his hands up with his palms toward the girls. "One question at a time. I saw the van at least three times.

It's always been going away from town, toward the country. Yes, and there're tons of places out on that road where Molly could be held."

"Should we tell the police?" Jackie asked.

"They probably won't believe us," Mandy said. "We're just kids, and grown-ups don't always believe what kids tell them. They think they're the only ones who know anything."

"Argo's not like that," Jenny said. "She'd probably help us."

"Would she let you go and look for the van?" Christy asked.

"Well…no. She'd say that it was too dangerous."

"Then don't tell her," Angie advised.

"What do you girls want to do?" Calvin asked.

"What if we rode our bikes out past your dad's house tomorrow morning," Jenny suggested. "No one would think anything of a bunch of kids riding their bikes on Saturday morning."

"I don't have a bike," Angie said.

"Marylou doesn't ride hers anymore," Jenny said. "She won't notice if you borrow it for the day."

"What's the plan?" Jackie asked.

"Let's meet at Calvin's house about ten o'clock," Jenny suggested. "We can put lunch in our backpacks, so we don't have to come back so soon."

"Sounds good," Susan said. "Can everyone go tomorrow?"

"I'm supposed to go to the grocery store with my dad," Mandy said, "but I can get out of that."

"Sounds good," Jenny said. "Everyone bring extra water."

"Why?" Angie asked.

"I always get thirsty when I ride my bike," Jenny said. "I just thought that everyone else would, too. Besides, if we find Molly, she might need some, too."

"Don't tell anyone where we're going," Susan cautioned in a low voice. She put her finger to her lips. "Someone will probably try and stop us."

"Okay," Calvin said. The others nodded their agreement. "Make sure your tires are pumped up. It'll make your bikes easier to ride. We might have to ride for a while, since I don't know exactly where the van goes."

With that, the club members walked up the stairs to ask if Mr. Jenkins would take them home. It was getting dark, and none of the girls wanted to be alone on the street at night after what had happened to Molly. They didn't want to be alone anywhere. Someone could snatch them, even if they didn't have any money.

Chapter Four

The next morning, after meeting at Calvin's house, The Lost Mothers' Club and Calvin rode out on Harrison Road. They stopped at Calvin's dad's house to rest and get a soda.

"Why did you kids ride your bikes way out here?" Mr. Kelly asked.

"We're just going for a ride, Dad," Calvin answered, not wanting to tell him the real reason.

Calvin introduced the girls to him, except for Jenny, whom he had already met.

"Well, at least you have good company," Mr. Kelly answered, winking at the girls. "I must say that you have good taste, Calvin."

Susan blushed, but the rest of the girls smiled. They drank the sodas that Calvin's dad gave them, then hopped on their bikes and rode down the driveway.

"Why did your mom and dad get a divorce?" Angie asked Calvin.

"My dad had a girlfriend, and my mom didn't like it."

"Oh." Angie couldn't think of anything else to say.

The group peddled on for almost a mile before Mandy spotted an old red barn. "Let's check that out," she said pointing to the building. Beyond the barn was an old farmhouse with peeling white paint.

"Okay," Jenny said, "but let's ride past the house and barn, then double back through the trees, in case anyone's watching. The trees will hide us until we're almost to the barn. Then, if we keep low, we can hide in the cornstalks until we get to the back of the barn."

"Sounds good," Calvin said. He had been around Jenny enough to trust her instincts.

Jenny led the way, stopping at the corner of the fence on the other side of the barn. She pushed her bike through a torn part of the fence and laid it down in the tall hay, hiding it from anyone passing by. The others did the same. Then the seven friends walked low in the hay, looking from side to side to see if anyone had noticed them. They saw no one. When they reached the barn, Christy found a loose board and pulled it aside. The gap she created was just large enough for them to squeeze through, if they sucked in their stomachs.

"I'll go in first," Calvin volunteered, "and check it out to see if anyone is in there." The girls were grateful. None of them wanted to be first. There could be spiders or other creepy crawlies waiting to squirm, squiggle, and wiggle all over the first person to enter. "I'll come back to let you know if it's clear," he promised.

After squeezing through the gap, Calvin lay flat on the floor and looked around. Christy had pulled the board back over the opening, so it was quite dark in the old barn. It took Calvin's eyes a good minute to adjust to the dim light. Warily, he climbed to his knees and looked around for some movement. He saw none. He cautiously stood up and looked some more from side to side and front to back. Something ran across his foot. He jumped straight up. When he landed, he saw a big rat running toward a horse stall in the corner. He crept over to the stall and peeked in. There, under an old green tarp, was a van. He knew it was white, because the tarp only partly covered it. He was so excited that he wanted to yell for the girls, but he knew that he had to be quiet. So he ran silently over to the loose board and called to the girls in a hoarse whisper. "Come on in, but be quiet. I found the van. Molly and the kidnappers must be inside the house." The girls crept in, one by one, each checking the floor for creepy crawlies.

"Are you sure it's the right van?" Susan asked.

"It has ice cream cones on the side," Calvin answered.

"Then we must be in the right place," Jenny reasoned. "The point is, now, what do we do about it?"

"We need to make a plan," Jackie said. She was really scared, but she didn't want the others to know. She tried to keep her voice even, to hide the trembling that she felt inside.

"Let's decide now," Jenny said. She sat down cross-legged on the barn floor and patted the floor for the others to sit, too. Calvin decided not to tell them about the rat. Everyone sat down, and several were glad to sit, for their knees were starting to shake from a combination of fear and excitement.

"We don't all need to run up to the house,"

Jenny said. "If we all go, there's more of a chance that we'll be seen."

Everyone agreed by solemnly nodding. The other girls didn't want to go anyway, if they could help it.

"I'll go, if someone else will go with me," Jenny volunteered. She loved adventure.

Calvin said, "I'll go with you, unless someone else wants to go."

The other girls all breathed a sigh of relief. They had all been holding their collective breath, afraid that they would be chosen to go up to the house. "Thanks," Susan said quietly.

"Yeah, thanks," the others chimed in.

"I'm not very brave," Angie admitted.

"Neither am I," Mandy said.

"Good, then it's all settled," Jenny said. She clapped her hands together. Excitement made her smile. "Calvin and I will go one at a time up to the bushes by the garden. We'll be able to see the side of the house from there." They got up and quietly ran to the door on the side of the barn. The others, not wanting to be left alone, followed.

Calvin peeked out the half-opened door and scanned the house and yard. He saw an open window with one pane broken out on the side of the house. Below the window were some overgrown azalea bushes. A small, scraggly tree grew up in the middle of the bushes, with a fork in the branches that was only a few feet from the ground. Calvin looked toward the back of the house and saw a man's leg jutting out over the porch. Billows of cigarette smoke floated over and away from the leg. From inside the house, he heard the sound of banging pots and pans. Calvin figured that someone was in the kitchen cooking, maybe the woman. He wondered where the third kidnapper and Molly were.

Calvin turned to Jenny and said, "If we run over to the bushes without being seen, we could climb the tree and look inside."

"What if one of the kidnappers was sitting on

the other side of the window?" Jenny asked. She liked to cover all possibilities.

"I'm scared," Jackie said, trembling.

"We all are," Christy said. She put her arm around Jackie's shoulder to comfort her. "But we need to stick together for Molly. Just imagine how scared she must be."

"If she's not dead already," Mandy said.

"Don't even think that." Jenny turned and put a hand on her left hip. She put the other hand on Mandy's shoulder and gave it a quick pat. "Think of her as being alive, and how we can help her." Her long, brown ponytail swung back and forth as she spoke, as if to give emphasis to her words.

Not one of the rescuers thought about running away from there and calling the police. Deep down they felt that if Molly was going to be rescued, they would have to do it, even if they were scared.

"What if someone created a diversion?" Jenny asked.

"What do you mean?" Mandy asked.

"Someone could go out in the woods," Jenny replied, "and make a noise, so the kidnappers would look out there and wouldn't see us run up to the house."

"What if the kidnappers ran out and caught us when we were making the noise?" Jackie asked.

"What if they have guns?" Mandy asked.

"What if they found us and tied us up, or killed us?" Susan asked. "We could be in as much trouble as Molly."

"What if we start a fire then ran back here to hide in the hay?" Angie asked. "The kidnappers would look toward the fire and not at us."

"What a great idea!" Jenny exclaimed. "Does anyone here have any matches?"

"No," Calvin answered, "but there might be some in the van. Someone's smoking on the back porch, so he may have left some matches or a lighter in the van."

"Mandy and I can look," Angie said. She took hold of Mandy's hand and ran toward the tarp-covered van. When they reached the van, Mandy pulled the cover up while Angie opened the driver's side door. "Look!" she squealed. "Here's Molly's shoe! She must have lost it when she was in the van." She picked up the shoe and stuck it under her belt at her back, then looked through the array of soda cans and fast food wrappers between the front seats. No lighter. Looking up, she spotted a lighter on the dashboard. She picked it up and tried to light it. It only sparked. She tried again. This time she saw a flame for only a second. The third time she flicked it, Angie was rewarded with a steady flame. "All right!" she squealed. "We're in business!" She backed out of the van and held the lighter up in triumph. She lit it again to show Mandy.

The girls ran back to the group standing by the door. Angie held up the lighter.

"All right!" Calvin said. He high-fived Angie. "There are plenty of old corn stalks in the field. You can pile them up in the middle and start a good fire. If you clear out the area around the pile, it shouldn't spread to the house or the barn. When the kidnappers go to investigate, Jenny and I can run up to the house."

With that, the five girls ran to the back of the barn and slipped out. They ran low between the corn stalks to the middle of the field, where they broke off the tall stalks and piled them up in a big stack. When they had a pile as high as the other corn stalks and as big around as a living room rug, Angie pulled the lighter out of her pocket and lit a dry leaf. She walked around the pile and lit it in seven different places. It soon blazed merrily, a smoky, hard-to-miss fire.

"Let's get out of here," Susan suggested She started running low toward the barn, with the others following close behind. They pulled back the loose board and slipped inside, panting.

Calvin and Jenny were still inside the barn looking at the house. They saw the man on the back porch jump up and run to the back door. He poked his head inside and yelled, "Fire!" Then he turned and ran toward the field. A woman and a man ran out the door after him, with their backs toward the barn.

"The coast is clear," Jenny said with excitement. "Let's go!"

Calvin and Jenny slipped out the barn door and ran low toward the bushes under the window. Jenny slipped behind the overgrown shrubs, while Calvin climbed into the tree and peeked in the window. He saw Molly lying on a dirty mattress. She was alive, but tied up. A rag was stuck in her mouth so she couldn't talk or yell. Her frightened eyes looked at Calvin, blinking furiously to keep back the tears. She tried to wiggle free, but she couldn't loosen the ropes. Calvin's eyes scanned the room. There was an old wooden chair in the corner and an open closet door behind Molly. No one else was in the room.

Calvin turned and looked down at Jenny. "Come on, before the kidnappers come back." He scrambled in the window while Jenny climbed the tree. She followed him in through the opening and gasped when she saw Molly.

Jenny ran to Molly and took the gag out of her mouth. "Poor, Molly," she said. She put her head down on Molly's cheek.

Molly started crying. "I'm so scared," she sobbed into Jenny's ear.

"The whole club is here to help you," Jenny said. "The others started a fire to get the kidnappers out of here, so we could come in and get you."

"The whole club?" Molly asked. She started crying again, only this time it was tears of gratitude. She couldn't believe that her friends had risked their lives to help her.

Calvin squatted down and worked on the ropes that were tied around Molly's hands. "Try to untie the ropes around her ankles," he told Jenny. Jenny tried to loosen the knots, but the kidnappers had done a thorough job when they tied her up. There were several knots around both her hands and feet. They had loosened only a few when Calvin heard voices.

"They're coming back!" Calvin hissed. "Quick, Jenny, we've got to hide!"

Chapter Five

"**L**ook!" Mandy exclaimed. "They're going back to the house." She pointed to the two men and the woman. "What if they find Jenny and Calvin?"

"Jenny's smart," Mandy said. "She'll know what to do."

"But those guys probably have guns," Jackie said.

"I'm scared," Susan said.

"Me, too," Angie said. "But we have to forget about being scared and think about helping our friends. We need to pull together."

"Okay, but what can we do?" Susan asked.

"We could start another fire," Angie suggested.

"Okay. Where?" Jackie asked.

"What about the old outhouse in the back yard. It's probably not used for anything anymore," Angie said. "My grandpa has one in his back yard, and he uses it to store rakes and stuff. We can get to it through the woods. Then there's just a short distance to the outhouse. One of us can run up to it from the back, so the kidnappers won't see whoever goes." She stopped and thought with her finger on her cheek. "We can take some hay from the barn to get the fire started."

"Sounds good," Jackie said. "That's the best idea I've heard." She bent over and gathered some hay off the barn floor. The others did the same.

They all ran out the broken part in the back of the barn, each carrying an armload of hay. They ducked through the cornstalks until they got to the woods, then they doubled around the yard through the trees until they got close to the outhouse.

* * * * * * * * *

While the girls were sneaking through the woods, Calvin and Jenny slipped into the closet and pulled the door partially shut, leaving Molly, now tied loosely, lying on the soiled mattress. Molly twisted her head around to see where they went and then turned her back to the bedroom doorway so the kidnappers wouldn't see that she didn't have the gag in her mouth. The woman walked down the wooden hallway floor and peered in the door to see if Molly was still there, then, satisfied, she went back to the kitchen. Molly heard someone move pots, pans, and dishes.

"Where did she go?" Jenny whispered to Calvin.

Calvin shrugged his shoulders.

"Where are the men?" she asked.

He shrugged his shoulders again.

"Let's sneak out and untie some more knots," Jenny whispered.

"It's too dangerous," Calvin whispered back. "Maybe the girls will create another diversion." He sat down and put his back against the closet wall. He looked down and found, stuck in the corner, a long forgotten hatpin. It looked like one of the straight pins his mom used when she sewed, only ten times longer. He picked it up and touched the point. It was still very sharp. He pinned it to the inside of his shirt, thinking that it might come in handy later.

Just then, Jenny and Calvin heard footsteps coming toward them on the bare wooden floor. Calvin pulled the door in a little more, and then he peeked out the crack. Jenny stood behind him, peering out above him, holding her breath.

"I wonder who started the fire," a man in an orange and white shirt asked.

"I don't know," the woman answered, "but I'm afraid it was done because someone knows we're here."

"How could they?" the man asked. "We were careful when we came here. No one followed us. I watched out the back window the whole time."

"Still," the woman answered, "someone could have seen the van in the barn."

"Who?" the man asked. He threw his hands into the air. "No one has come up the lane since we've been here. Kids from the next farm were probably playing with matches and set the fire." He turned and went back down the hall. The woman walked partly into the room, glanced at Molly and whispered, "Well, my little rich girl. You're going to make me a very wealthy woman when your father brings the money. I'll be out of the country with all of it before they find you. Maybe you'll live, and maybe you won't. My friends won't survive long enough to spend any of it. I've got plans for them." She rubbed her hands together and turned abruptly, then walked out of the room.

"Whew!" Jenny whispered as she let out her breath in a big gush. "I'm glad they didn't notice that the closet door was closed."

"Me, too," Calvin whispered. He opened the door a little wider and winked at Molly. "We'll be out of here soon," he promised in a low voice.

A tear slid down Molly's cheek. She was so frightened, frightened for her life, and now frightened for the lives of her friends. The woman scared her. Was she going to kill the men? Would she kill her before she left with the money? Would she kill her friends because they tried to help her? She tried to wiggle the ropes loose. The knots around her hands gave away, just a little, but enough to give her hope. She wiggled her feet, but the knots remained tight. She began to cry softly. She prayed silently, "Please, God, let us get out of here alive." More tears slid down her cheeks and wet the mattress under her face.

Chapter Six

Calvin looked toward the bedroom door and was about to step out when Jenny pulled him back. "Wait," she hissed. "It's too dangerous. Maybe the girls will create another diversion."

They waited in silence, listening for any sounds that would tell them where the kidnappers were or what the girls were doing. They heard pots and pans clamoring in the kitchen. They heard the back screen door slam shut, but they didn't know if anyone went out or came in from the back porch.

They wondered where the girls were and if they had thought of something else to get the kidnappers out of the house.

Molly was still crying quietly. Jenny could see her tears. Her heart hurt for Molly, but for the moment she couldn't help her. If she got caught, she would be of no help to Molly. They both would be tied up, or worse.

* * * * * * * * *

Meanwhile, the girls on the outside had run through the woods to the back of the house, directly behind the outhouse. "Who's going to start the fire this time?" Susan asked.

"I will," Angie said bravely, "unless one of you really wants to do it."

"No, that's all right," Susan said. She didn't want to leave the safety of the woods.

"You can do it," Mandy said. She also wanted to stay hidden.

The girls all handed their hay to Angie. It was piled on her arms up past her nose, so she could hardly see over it. Susan pushed the pile down in front of Angie's face, so she could see to walk. Angie put her chin on the hay to hold it down and stepped to the edge of the woods. She looked over the backyard. The back porch was hidden from her view by the outhouse, so she figured that if she couldn't see anyone, they couldn't see her. Angie bravely walked straight to the back of the old outhouse and threw down the hay. She stuffed it all around the edges and piled the rest up against the rotting boards. The wood was old and dried out, almost like kindling. Angie stuffed some hay between the loose boards, then pulled the lighter out of her jeans pocket. She lit the dry hay in three places, then turned and raced back to the woods. As soon as the foliage safely hid her, the five girls ran back to the barn and slipped inside. Mandy tripped over a fallen branch on the way, but she scrambled up in a panic, afraid to be left behind.

* * * * * * * *

Calvin and Jenny were still waiting in the closet, peeking through the crack of the door, listening for clues as to what the kidnappers were doing. A radio was playing country music. Jenny smelled bacon cooking. Her mouth watered. She loved bacon. She glanced at Molly, who was licking her dry, cracked lips. "Poor Molly," she whispered. "She looks so thirsty." Jenny wished she hadn't left her water bottle strapped to her bike.

A man's voice suddenly yelled from the back porch. "Fire! There's another fire!"

Jenny, Calvin, and Molly heard the woman and the man that were in the house run toward the back door. The door banged open, and the footsteps went out onto the porch. It was now or never to save Molly. They slipped out of the closet and worked on Molly's ropes. Calvin finished the job on Molly's wrists and then helped Jenny with her feet. The ropes finally slipped free from Molly's feet. Jenny helped her to stand and immediately shoved her toward the window. Calvin scrambled out first and helped Molly through the window. Jenny quickly climbed out after Molly and joined her friends behind the bushes. They rolled under the bushes as far as they could, so the kidnappers wouldn't find them.

The man in the orange and white shirt found a water hose and turned it on. He wet the grass around the outhouse, so the fire wouldn't spread to the house. The woman yelled, "I told you someone knew we were here!"

"It was probably the kids from next door again," the man answered. "I used to do things like that when I was a teenager." He continued to water the ground, occasionally squirting the outhouse. The other man and the woman watched the old outhouse burn merrily, mesmerized by the sight. They temporarily forgot about Molly and the cooking bacon.

The woman happened to glance back at the house. "Oh, my gosh!" she yelled. "Now, the house is on fire!" She ran back to the house and raced up the back steps. Both men ran after her. The kitchen wall by the stove flamed. The forgotten bacon grease had ignited and set the old, peeling wallpaper behind the stove on fire. Flames were licking the ceiling and the old dry cupboards.

"Bring the hose in here!" the woman yelled to the man in the orange and white shirt.

"Get the girl!" the other man yelled.

"Let her burn," the woman said. "We'll still get our money. Her father won't know she's dead."

Calvin, Jenny, and Molly heard this conversation from their hiding place under the bushes.

Molly shuddered. She thought that she would have really been burned up if Calvin and Jenny hadn't helped her out of the house.

"Let's run to the barn while they're putting out the fire," Jenny suggested. "This is as good a chance as we're going to get."

Calvin and Molly both nodded and rose to their knees. They peeked out over the bushes to see if anyone was looking, then they rose to their feet. "You go first," Calvin said to Jenny, "and take Molly with you. I'll come in a minute."

Jenny nodded and grabbed hold of Molly's arm. "Let's go," she whispered. Together they ran toward the barn, Jenny practically pulling Molly. Molly was so weak that she could hardly walk by herself. The girls in the barn opened the door a crack to let them in, then shut it quickly behind them.

"Oh, Molly," Angie said. "I'm so glad you're safe. We were so-oo worried."

"Me, too," Molly answered. "Thanks you guys for setting the fires."

"It's the only thing we could think to do," Christy answered.

"Look what I've got," Angie said. She pulled Molly's shoe from under her belt. "I found it in the van."

"My shoe!" Molly said. She reached out and took it. "Thanks. It was hard running through the rocky yard with only one shoe." She sat down and pulled the shoe on her foot. "Where's Calvin? He should be here by now." Molly sounded worried.

"Those people are really mean, especially the woman."

Jackie peeked out the door. "Here he comes," she announced. "Let's go out the back and be ready to run when he comes." She looked over by the back of the house. "Oh, no! We won't have time. Hide! One of the men saw Calvin."

Chapter Seven

Calvin ran as fast as his legs could carry him. He burst through the barn door and tripped over an old shovel, falling flat on his stomach, skinning his knee in the process.

Jenny ran to him and helped him up. "Are you all right?" she asked, concern in her voice.

"Sure," Calvin said bravely, even though his knee was bleeding. "Quick, everyone, hide! They saw me."

"Where?" Christy asked.

"Over there," Calvin said, pointing to an old horse stall below the hayloft.

Once in the stall, the children discovered a ladder hidden behind a short wall going up to the loft.

Angie started climbing as fast as she could. "Follow me, but be quiet," she cautioned. Christy and Mandy climbed up after her.

The other girls and Calvin didn't have time to escape into the loft before the kidnappers burst through the big barn door. "Lie flat and cover up with hay," Calvin whispered. "It's dark in here, so they might not see us."

Susan, Molly, Jenny, and Jackie followed Calvin's instructions, flattening out and pulling dirty hay over them as fast as they could. They all backed up to the barn wall and lay perfectly still, not daring to even breathe loud. Jenny's heart was pounding so hard, she was afraid the kidnappers would hear it. Calvin needed to sneeze because of the dusty hay, so he pinched his finger under his nose to stop it. His knee hurt, but he couldn't think about that right now. He knew they'd be dead if they were caught.

The three girls in the loft saw two men burst through the door. Angie gasped. "Lie down flat so they won't see you," she hissed to Christy and Mandy. Christy and Mandy plopped down, trying to be as quiet as possible. The three girls watched in horror as the men looked around, waiting for their eyes to adjust to the darkness of the barn.

"Where did they go?" the man in the orange shirt asked.

"I don't know," the other man said. "Maybe they went out the back."

"There's no door," the man in the orange shirt said.

"Maybe there's a loose board they could have slipped through. I'll go around and look in the field behind the barn."

"Okay," the man in the orange shirt said. "But if you don't see them, come back and help me." He waved the gun in his hand toward the door. "Kathy went back to make sure the fire is out, so I'll need you to help." He turned and walked toward the horse stall where the white van was parked. Angie let out a sigh of relief that he wasn't going toward the stall where her friends were and where the ladder was hidden.

Once he was out of sight of the children hiding in the hay, Calvin whispered, "See if there's a loose board back here. We can escape after the other man checks out the field."

The girls brushed off some of the hay and felt the barn wall behind them. No luck. Everything was tightly nailed. Calvin felt behind him and was rewarded with a rotten board that he could punch his fist through, right at the bottom where the wall met the floor. He stopped after the first punch, fearing that the kidnapper in the back would hear him.

Meanwhile, in the hayloft, Christy spied a broken pitchfork handle. She pulled it over and held it close, thinking that she might be able to use it to defend herself. She didn't think about the fact that the kidnappers had guns, and that a broken handle would hardly be of any help.

Angie spied a big rock a few feet from her. She inched over and grabbed it, just as the kidnapper in the orange shirt came out of the stall that hid the van. He walked toward the other stalls, stopping once to look in the big covered box that once held oats. Jenny was thankful that she hadn't hidden in the box, for she knew that the man would have shot her if he'd found her in there. She breathed a silent prayer of "Thank you."

The man in the orange shirt was heading toward the stall where the girls and Calvin were hiding, when the other man rushed in through the big barn door. "They aren't out back," he said breathlessly. "I checked the cornfield, and no one was there."

"Well, they have to be in here, then," orange shirt answered. "You take this side." He pointed toward the stall where Calvin and the girls were hiding. "I'll take this ladder up to the loft."

"Oh, no!" Angie whispered. "There's another ladder." Without really thinking, she stood up and hurled the rock in her hand across the barn, clear to the far wall, where it hit with a big 'Thunk.' She was thankful that she was the girls' softball pitcher, for it had strengthened her arm.

"What was that?" the man in the orange shirt yelled. "They must be over there!" He spun around quickly and bumped his arm on one of the barn support posts, discharging his gun.

BANG!

The other man screamed. "You dummy! You shot me!" He dropped down on the floor and wrapped his hands around his violently bleeding leg. The man with the gun pulled off his orange shirt and tied it around the other man's leg to help stop the bleeding.

With all the commotion, neither of the men heard Calvin punch out the rotten board in the back of the barn. When he had punched out a hole just big enough for him to wiggle out, he stopped and motioned for Jenny to get Molly out of there. He scrambled quietly up the ladder to get the other girls, while those in the horse stall escaped. Angie, Christy, and Mandy practically slid down the ladder after Calvin, with Mandy still holding the broken pitchfork handle. Christy and Angie wormed their way out the small opening. Mandy and Calvin were next, but maybe too late. They heard the kidnapper, now shirtless, running toward them.

"Quick, Mandy! Get out!" Calvin hissed. Mandy slid through the opening, still holding her broken pitchfork handle, and waited for Calvin. The other girls ran through the cornfield toward their bicycles, not daring to look back.

Just as Calvin slid through the small opening, a bloody hand, decorated with a tattooed snake, reached out and grabbed his foot. Mandy surprised even herself when she stepped forward with the broken handle and, with all her strength, hit the arm that was holding Calvin. The man screamed and cursed at Mandy. The hand loosened just enough for Calvin to break free and scramble to his feet.

"Thanks," he muttered.

"That's okay," Mandy smiled. Her smile faded when she saw a head come out of the opening. The shirtless kidnapper was trying to squirm through. She hit his head with the handle, hard.

"You little brat!" the man screamed. "I'll get you for this!" He looked at Mandy with the meanest look that she'd ever seen.

"You'll have to catch me first!" she taunted. Mandy broke into a run. "Com'on, Calvin!"

"Just a minute. He's not going anywhere, not for the moment, anyway."

Mandy stopped and turned around. Sure enough, the man's wide shoulders were stuck in the little hole. One of his hands, the one with the gun, was still on the other side of the wall. Calvin reached into his shirt and pulled out the big hatpin he stuck there while he was hiding in the closet. He held it up and plunged it deep into the kidnapper's shoulder. The man screamed in pain. If he tried to pull back through the hole into the barn, the pin would be driven deeper into his shoulder and tear through his flesh. The man couldn't slither out through the opening because of his fat stomach, and he couldn't slither back because of the pin. He was really stuck.

"You little monster!" the man shouted. "Just wait until I get out of here. I'll get you good!" He acted tough, but he had tears in his eyes from the pain of the pin. Calvin almost felt sorry for him.

"Let's go," he said to Mandy. He grabbed her hand and pulled her away, even though the sight of the big tough guy with tears in his eyes fascinated her.

The two friends ran through the cornfield toward their bikes. The other girls were already there, pulling up their handlebars, ready to flee as soon as Calvin and Mandy reached them.

"Where are they?" Christy asked. "They should be here by now."

"I'm worried," Susan said.

"Me, too," Jackie agreed.

"Don't worry," Jenny tried to reassure her

friends. "Calvin can take care of Mandy as well as himself." She said this with confidence, but deep down, she was worried, too.

Suddenly a shot rang out. BANG! Someone was shooting a gun.

"Oh, no!" Angie yelled. "Someone's shooting at us!"

Chapter Eight

Jenny's head jerked around toward the shot. "The shots aren't for us!" she yelled. "Look!" The woman kidnapper stood on the other side of the field. She was standing with her legs spread apart and her arms held straight out, aiming the gun at Calvin. "Quick, everyone, scream as loud as you can!" Jenny ordered.

No one asked why. They all knew that Jenny had good instincts, and if she said to scream, they'd scream.

Six girls screamed at the top of their lungs. The sound was deafening. It was enough for the woman to look over at them and temporarily forget about Calvin and Mandy. She turned toward the girls, aimed the gun, and shot. The six girls hit the ground just as a shot passed over them.

"Whew!" Angie exclaimed. "That was close. At least she didn't hit Mandy and Calvin."

"Quick!" Jenny said. "Crawl over to the ditch and cover yourselves with leaves." Again, the five friends didn't question Jenny. They just did it.

Another shot rang out. BANG! This time it was aimed at Mandy and Calvin. Fortunately, the woman wasn't a good shot and missed them by several feet. The two friends ran as fast as they had never run before. Their feet pounded the soft dirt in record time as they ran, not daring to look around and see where the woman was.

Jenny peered up from the ditch and saw the woman run after Calvin. After a few feet into the field, the kidnapper stepped into a gully and twisted her ankle. She fell flat on her face, while the gun sailed several feet away from her hand.

"Let's get her!" Jenny yelled. With a whoop and a holler, she jumped out of the ditch and ran toward the sprawled out woman. Calvin and Mandy saw Jenny run and they turned around. Calvin was closer to the kidnapper than Jenny was, so he ran for the gun, with Mandy right behind him. Just as the woman crawled over and put her hand on the gun, Calvin kicked it away, hurting the woman's hand in the process.

"Good one, Calvin!" Mandy yelled as she ran up and slapped him on the back.

By this time, Jenny and Angie caught up to Calvin and Mandy. Calvin picked up the gun and pointed it at the woman, while Jenny, Angie, and Mandy sat on her.

"Get off me, you little creeps," the woman hissed through clenched teeth. "I'll get you for this!"

"Not by the hair of my chinny-chin-chin," Jenny said. "You can't get rid of us that easily. You were mean to our friend. You probably were going to kill her. Why should we let you up?"

The other girls, breathless, ran up to Calvin. "Where's the other guy?" Christy asked. "I know one was shot in the barn, but where's the other one?"

"He's stuck in the hole in the barn," Calvin said proudly. "I made sure he'd stay there with a big pin I found in the closet."

"How'd you do that?" Jenny looked confused.

Calvin quickly explained. "I rammed the pin into his shoulder, so he couldn't back up. His stomach was too big to get through the hole the other way, so he's stuck." Jackie made a face and put her hand to her mouth. Just thinking about a pin stuck in his shoulder made her stomach queasy.

"Good one, Calvin," Jenny said with a smile.

"What can we do?" Susan asked.

"Go get help!" Jenny yelled from her position on the kidnappers back. "And hurry!" The girls turned and ran for their bikes as fast as they could.

"Where do we go from here?" Susan asked when they arrived at the place they had dropped their bikes.

"Let's go to that old red farmhouse we passed coming here," Christy suggested.

"Okay," Jackie said. She looked at Molly and said, "You take Jenny's bike."

"Which one is it?" Molly asked.

Jackie pointed over to the red bike on the edge of the field. "That one."

Susan was already running her bike over to the road by the time Molly picked up Jenny's bike. She was in a hurry to get out of the field, to get to someplace safe, and to get someone to help her friends. Jackie, Molly, and Christy followed Susan down the street and up the driveway of the big red farmhouse down the road.

"Look! There's a car and a truck in the driveway," Christy said. "That must mean there's someone home."

"I hope they'll help us." Jackie said in a worried tone. "I hope they're nice, and not like the kidnappers." She put her bike down in the grass beside the driveway.

"Don't even think like that," Susan said. "I'm scared enough already." She plopped her bike down next to Jackie's.

"Watch out!" Molly yelled. A big black dog ran around the corner of the house, rapidly coming toward the girls. It was bigger than any of the girls.

"That's one big dog," Christy said. "Do you think he'll bite?"

Suddenly Jackie stopped and smiled.

"What are you grinning at?" Susan asked.

"Greta."

"Greta? Who's that?" Susan asked.

"Greta's the dog," she answered. "Here, Greta! Here, girl!" she called. The big dog ran over to

Jackie and stood eyeball to eyeball, while she licked Jackie's face.

"You know this dog?" Susan asked in amazement.

"Sure. This is Claudia's dog, Greta." When she heard her name, Greta licked Jackie across her cheek, from her nose to her ear.

"Who's Claudia?" Susan asked.

"My babysitter," Jackie answered. "I knew she lived out here someplace, but I didn't know which house."

"How do you know Greta?"

"Claudia brought her to my house a couple of times," Jackie answered. "This must be where she lives. That's her new truck over there." She broke into a run, with Greta at her heels, and called, "Claudia! Help! Claudia!"

Sixteen-year-old Claudia looked out an upstairs window and saw four girls running toward her house. She recognized Jackie, but she didn't know the others. Curious, she turned and ran out of her bedroom and down the stairs. She arrived at the door the same time the girls reached it. Claudia flung the door open and asked, "Jackie, what's the matter?"

"Someone kidnapped Molly, and we rescued her!" Jackie yelled so quickly that Claudia could hardly understand her.

"Slow down, Jackie, and say that again," Claudia said.

"I said," Jackie said impatiently, "that someone kidnapped Molly and held her at the farmhouse next door. We rescued her."

"You rescued her?" Claudia asked. She looked confused.

"Well, we had Jenny, Calvin, Mandy, and Angie to help us."

"Where are they?" Claudia asked.

"Next door, sitting on the woman kidnapper," Jackie said. "Calvin is holding a gun on her."

"Wait! This is too much for me," Claudia said. "Start over and tell me what's going on." She looked at Molly and asked, "Aren't you the one who's been on the TV news?"

"We'll tell you all about it," Jackie promised. "But, please, first call the police, or let me do it."

"Okay, I'll call, but you have to tell them what happened." Claudia walked into her house and picked up the cordless phone in the front hall. She punched in 9-1-1 and then handed the phone to Jackie.

Chapter Nine

Within minutes, police sirens could be heard in the distance. As they drew closer, the girls could see four police cars with lights flashing and sirens screaming. All four screeched around the corner of Claudia's driveway and skidded to a stop a few feet from the girls. Claudia's mom heard the commotion and ran up from the basement, where she was doing laundry. She was shocked to see four police cars and eight policemen in her driveway. Greta was circling, sniffing everyone and everything she could put her nose to.

"Will the dog bite?" one nervous policeman asked Claudia's mother.

"She never has yet."

"Well, I'd feel better if you put her up. She's pretty big."

Claudia's mother called Greta and put her in the house. By the time she turned around, the girls in her yard were telling the policemen a wild story about a kidnapping and pointing to the farmhouse next door. She recognized Molly from all the pictures that had been on the television news in the past few days.

One policeman pushed his hat back on his head and scratched his bald spot. "You mean to tell me that you kids rescued Molly? We've been looking for her for days."

"Yes, yes," Jackie said impatiently. "Our friends are still in danger over there with the kidnappers."

"Get in my police car and show us where they are," the policeman said quickly. He pointed to the first police car. The girls ran for the back door and slipped in, pushing each one over as they got in. Two policemen jumped in the front seat, turned on their siren and sped off. Jackie and Susan struggled to get on their seat belts, while Christy and Molly pulled the middle seat belt around both of them. The other police cars sped after them, kicking up dirt and stones as they turned the corner onto the road. Claudia and her mom watched with awe.

"Stop here!" Christy yelled after only a moment. "Our friends are over there."

The two policemen looked into the field in amazement. They saw a young boy pointing a big gun at a woman on the ground, while three girls sat on her back, one at the neck, one on her waist, and one on her legs.

The girls rapidly told the two policemen about the wounded man in the barn and about the one stuck in the wall. The policeman in the driver's seat radioed the other three police cars. He told them about the other two kidnappers and their location. "We've got this situation under control; just collect the other two scumbags. Make sure you read them their rights."

The rest of the police cars tore up the driveway to the old barn and skidded to a stop, one at the barn door and the other two on the sides of the barn. Two policemen drew their guns and ran into the barn, while the other policemen circled around the barn from the sides. They had their guns drawn and pointed them straight-ahead, stopping at each corner to flatten themselves out before they rounded the corner. The two men were apprehended without a struggle, for they were hurting too badly to put up much of a fight.

Meanwhile, Jackie led the first two policemen to the woman kidnapper.

"Give me the gun, son," one of the policemen said to Calvin.

"Okay. I was afraid to shoot it anyway," he admitted. "I didn't want to hurt any of the girls."

"Now you tell me," the woman kidnapper muttered.

Jenny laughed. "You still couldn't run off, not with us sitting on you."

One of the policemen pulled handcuffs from his belt and slapped them on the woman's wrists before she could get up. "You have the right to remain silent. Anything you say can and will be used against you in a court of law. You have the right to have an attorney. If you cannot afford an attorney, one will be appointed for you. Do you understand these rights?"

"You girls and your friend here," the other policeman pointed at Calvin, "certainly are brave. I'm impressed."

"Thanks," Calvin said. A big smile crossed his face.

"I really mean it," the policeman said. "You captured three bad people without any weapons."

"Oh, we had weapons," Jenny said happily.

"Angie had a rock, Mandy had a pitchfork handle, and Calvin had a big long pin."

"That's unbelievable," the policeman said. "Those people had guns."

"They couldn't shoot straight, though," Jenny said.

"Yes! Thank goodness for that!" Mandy exclaimed.

"Well, we need you to come down to the police station and tell us the whole story. You can call your families from there." He radioed back to the police station, told the dispatcher the good news, and asked him to call Molly's dad. "Tell him we'll be there in about ten minutes and reassure him that Molly is all right, thanks to her brave friends."

Calvin and the girls smiled at what the policeman said. They were proud of themselves. They had done what grown-ups weren't able to do. They had rescued Molly.

Angie glanced over toward the barn. "Look!"

she said, as she pointed to one of the police cars. Calvin and the other girls turned in time to see a policeman shove the shirtless man into the back of one of the squad cars. Blood was streaming down his back from the wound made by the pin. He had struggled to get out of the hole and had torn a good part of his shoulder doing it, but he was still stuck there when the police found him.

Jackie asked the policeman, "May we drop off the rest of our bikes at Claudia's house next door before we go? She'll take care of them until we get back."

"Sure," the policeman said. "We'll pick you up over there."

Jenny, Jackie, and Calvin took the remaining bikes and pedaled over to Claudia's house, while the rest of the girls climbed into the police cars. Jackie wanted to tell Claudia about what had happened next door before they went with the police. Just as they turned into Claudia's driveway, an ambulance and a Crime Scene Investigation Unit sailed past them, sirens blaring and lights flashing. Channel

Two and Channel Eleven news trucks followed close behind.

"Cool!" Calvin said. "News trucks. Maybe we'll be famous."

"I don't care if we're famous or not," Jenny said. "I'm just glad that Molly's safe."

"Me, too," Jackie agreed, "but it would be fun to be on the news."

Claudia ran out to meet Jenny, Calvin, and Jackie. "This is so awesome! You're going to be so famous. Everyone will know what you did. I can't believe I know someone who captured kidnappers."

While the friends waited for the policemen to come and pick them up, they told Claudia all about how they found Molly and how they helped her escape. Claudia looked horrified when they told her about how one kidnapper shot the other one and how the woman shot at them. She laughed when she heard what Calvin had done with the pin. "Way to go, Calvin!" Calvin looked pleased.

The ambulance screamed past Claudia's house. The children could see both the men in the back with a policeman and a paramedic.

"I guess the police didn't want either of them to bleed all over their police cars," Calvin said.

Three police cars came out of the kidnappers' driveway and rolled down the road to Claudia's house. The news trucks followed them right up the driveway. A woman with a microphone and a man with a camera jumped out of the Channel Two news van, and two men jumped out of the other. All four of them ran for the three children, but a policeman pushed them out of the way and tucked the children into the nearest police car. The cameramen filmed them through the back window as the police car sped away. Calvin turned around with a smile and waved.

Chapter Ten

The police talked to the Lost Mothers' Club and Calvin for almost two hours. They were amazed that the children could do what the police couldn't... find Molly. Then, most amazing of all, they rescued her.

Sergeant Anderson, the policeman in charge of Molly's investigation, was somewhat embarrassed about the whole situation. He thought that the police would be able to find Molly, not some kids on their first try. After all, they were supposed to be the professionals, the ones with training in police matters, the ones trained in investigations. But, in spite of it all, he was also very impressed with how they had freed Molly and captured the kidnappers without any weapons.

Calvin happily told what had happened. He was proud of himself. He was proud of the girls, how they had helped, even if they were scared. They didn't back down in time of crisis. They did what they had to do to free Molly. They had all worked together as a team, each doing their part.

The girls were questioned, but each story was the same as Calvin's, so the police thought it was time to take the children home. Molly was already at home with her dad. Sergeant Mary Paul, the only woman on the Summerville Police force, questioned her there. She was quiet and kind in her questioning, for she knew that Molly had several rough days with the kidnappers. She knew that she had been afraid, afraid of what the kidnappers were going to do to her and afraid that she might die.

Molly sat in her father's lap and answered

Sergeant Paul's questions. Her father's face had tears streaming down his cheeks. He had been so scared for Molly, afraid that he might never see his little girl again. He was thankful to have her back, thankful to be able to hold her again, thankful for the second chance to love her.

Calvin and the girls had been assured that the kidnappers were locked up and would stay locked up, so they didn't have to worry about them. Sergeant Anderson told them, "We're going to need all of you to testify in court to make sure these people stay in jail. You'll have to tell what happened in front of a lot of people in court: a judge, jury, lawyers, and the kidnappers. We'll be there to protect you, and the kidnappers will be well guarded."

"You mean I'll have to put my hand on a Bible and swear to tell the truth and nothing but the truth like they do on TV?" Calvin asked with a smile on his face. He loved to be the center of attention.

Sergeant Anderson smiled. "That's right. Can you do that?"

"You bet! This is going to be so cool!"

"Can you girls do that?" Sergeant Anderson asked. He looked over at the girls, sitting together on a long wooden bench.

All the girls all nodded, but they weren't as sure as Calvin. They were a little scared to talk in front of so many people, especially if they were face to face with the kidnappers. It was one thing to do what was needed in the heat of the moment while they were rescuing Molly. It would be another thing entirely to calmly tell their story in front of a large group of staring grown-ups.

The parents of the children had been called as soon as the Lost Mothers' Club and Calvin had arrived at the police station. One by one they rushed in to make sure that their child was all right. Each parent was relieved that their child was not harmed, and, after hugging them, had taken a seat on the other side of the room while the children were questioned.

Mr. Jenkins, Jenny's dad, sat next to Calvin's mother. They talked quietly, amazed and proud of their children, but worried, too, that they had taken such a chance. "When I think of the danger they put themselves in, I shudder," Mr. Jenkins said. "Jenny is a little headstrong, but I don't think she's ever put herself in so much danger before." Calvin's mom nodded. She had been worried, also, worried about losing Calvin. The kidnappers could have killed him.

Finally, it was soon time to leave. Mr. Jenkins had come in his pickup truck, so he offered to get the bicycles and drop them off at everyone's house. Calvin begged his mom, "Let me ride with Jenny! I'll help them get the bikes." She knew he'd be in good hands, so she hugged him and said that she'd see him later.

Once outside, the Lost Mothers' Club and Calvin had microphones pushed into their faces by very aggressive reporters. The reporters were shouting questions, each trying to be louder than the others. Light flashes and video cameras were everywhere, as photographers tried to take pictures of all the children.

"How did you capture the kidnappers?" one reporter yelled.

"How did you know where Molly was?" another reporter shouted.

"Were you scared?" another reporter yelled.

Mr. Jenkins tried to get past them, pushing forward with Jenny and Calvin, but the reporters blocked their way. He finally said, "If it's all right with the police and their investigation, we can hold a news conference tomorrow afternoon. But, please, let these children go home now. They've been through a lot today."

"This is so cool," Calvin smiled. "Just think - - a news conference. We're going to be famous!" He raised his hands above his head and jumped down the last three steps in front of the police station.

Mr. Jenkins smiled. "We'll only have a news conference if the police say it's all right. Besides, I really don't think that it's too safe to put you kids in the spotlight. What if the kidnappers have friends or family that might come after you? If you go on the Five O'clock News, the whole country will see you, and that could put you kids in danger." The parents of the other children behind Mr. Jenkins nodded their heads in agreement. They felt that their children had been in enough danger already.

By that time, several policemen had seen the reporters and held them back, so the parents and the children could get through. They arrived safely at their cars, but several reporters ran over to the vehicles and started taking pictures of the children as they were leaving.

"That was fun!" Jenny exclaimed. She pressed her nose against the window and watched the reporters.

"Yeah!" Calvin smiled. "This is so cool."

"It won't be cool if someone recognizes you and comes after you," Mr. Jenkins said soberly. "I hope they didn't get my license tag in their pictures."

"Why?" Jenny asked.

"They can find out who owns the truck through

the Department of Motor Vehicles, and then the reporters might show up at our house."

"Argo will shoo them away." Jenny said. "She won't let them come into the yard."

Mr. Jenkins smiled at the thought of Argo running out of the house waving a dishtowel chasing the reporters away. Then again, Argo was a formidable woman, and Mr. Jenkins wouldn't want her mad at him. "True, but the rest of the families don't have an Argo to protect them. The reporters could have taken pictures of the other cars as well."

They drove to Claudia's house in silence, Jenny and Calvin both thinking over what Mr. Jenkins said. True, they would like to be famous, but they wanted to be alive as well. If someone could come after them for revenge because of what they did to the kidnappers, then being famous wasn't worth it.

Claudia was sitting on her front porch when Mr. Jenkins drove up. She ran out to meet them. "Hey, you guys! You're famous! You were just on the news!"

"We were?" Calvin asked.

"Yeah, there was a newsbreak in the movie I was watching. It showed you kids coming out of the police station, and Mr. Jenkins talking about a news conference tomorrow."

"That was on the news?" Mr. Jenkins looked startled.

"It sure was," Claudia answered.

"Uh, oh!" Mr. Jenkins said. "I'm sure the reporters know who some of you kids are already, or maybe all of you. It's going to be tough dodging them now."

"I put your bikes in the garage," Claudia said. "Some crew from Channel Five drove up into the driveway and took pictures them."

"Thanks," Jenny said. She hugged Claudia and ran for the garage. Calvin hopped into the bed of the truck as Mr. Jenkins sat down in the driver's seat. By the time they drove over to the garage, Jenny already had one bike out. Mr. Jenkins lifted the bike up to Calvin, and he stowed it crosswise behind the window. In no time at all, all seven bikes were in the truck, and Jenny and Calvin were on their way. Mr. Jenkins looked worried as they drove home, thinking of the reporters and the danger Jenny and her friends could be in.

Chapter Eleven

Calvin saw them first. "Look! He pointed to several news vans in front of Calvin's and Jenny's houses. When they drove up, a reporter ran up to the truck and poked a microphone through the driver's side window.

She looked at Calvin and Jenny and asked, "How does it feel to be heroes?"

Mr. Jenkins pushed the microphone away and said, "No comment. Please leave my property."

The reporter poked the microphone back into the truck. "I understand these two young people saved their friend, Molly, from her kidnappers."

"We didn't do it by ourselves," Jenny said. "We had help."

"Hush, Jenny," Mr. Jenkins said. He turned to the reporter and said, "Please leave my property, or I will call the police." He drove into the garage and pushed the remote to close the door. The reporter stood under the door to make it go back up. "Leave now!" Mr. Jenkins said. The reporter just stood there waiting for them to get out of the truck. Mr. Jenkins blew the truck's horn, loud, three times.

Argo opened the adjoining door to the kitchen. She immediately grasped the problem and reached for the phone just inside the door. She punched in 9-1-1 and told the dispatcher about the brazen reporter. Minutes later, a siren could be heard coming down the street. Then, and only then, the reporter reluctantly left the Jenkins' yard and went to stand by the news van at the end of the driveway. A police car drove up. One policeman walked over to the reporter, and the other walked up the driveway to the garage.

"What's the problem here?" asked the second policeman.

"The media won't leave us alone," Mr. Jenkins explained as he stepped out of the truck. "The woman standing by the van wouldn't leave when I asked her to, and she tried to follow me into my garage. These kids have gone through enough today. They don't need to be harassed by reporters."

"I agree," the policeman said. "I'll go and talk to them. If necessary, I'll try to get a temporary restraining order to keep them away, that is, if you'll agree."

"By all means," Mr. Jenkins said. "Maybe all this attention will die down, but for now, it's very annoying."

"I think it's cool," Calvin piped up. He slid under the steering wheel and jumped down to the garage floor.

"Me, too," Jenny said, following Calvin.

"It could be dangerous for you if too many people know who you are," the policeman said.

"That's what I told them earlier," Mr. Jenkins said.

"For tonight, and probably tomorrow, try to stay out of sight as much as possible," the policeman said. "Where does the young man live?"

"Next door," Jenny volunteered. She pointed to Calvin's house. "Mandy lives across the street, but the other girls all live a few blocks from here."

"It would be well for all of you to lay low for a while, for your own safety." The policeman turned and walked down the driveway.

Calvin's mom heard the commotion outside and walked over to the Jenkins' house. Argo invited her in, and the grown-ups talked while Calvin and Jenny told Marylou everything that had happened. Argo called Jenny over to the adults and asked her to call her friends and tell them what the policeman said about staying out of sight.

"We can do that," Jenny said. "Com'on, Calvin, we have to make some calls."

Jenny threw the kitchen cordless phone to Calvin and picked up the other cordless from the living room. She punched in the numbers and signaled when Calvin could listen in. At every house, the story was the same. There were reporters harassing all the families of her friends from The Lost Mothers' Club. Susan had even let it slip about their club and why they went to look for Molly.

The next morning, the Sunday paper's headlines read BRAVE CLUB MEMBERS RESCUE FRIEND. There was a big story about the kidnapping and how the children had rescued Molly. It seemed that the reporters had gotten together and compared notes. They had put together a story compiled from small things that each of the children had said. They had even interviewed Claudia. The television news was much the same. The children were heroes, but they were also prisoners, prisoners in their own homes. If they went out, they either had to hide on the floorboards of their cars to get past the reporters or stay inside.

* * * * * * * * * *

Argo insisted that the Jenkins family was not going to be treated like prisoners. She made Sunday morning breakfast and announced that they were going to church. "I'll take care of those reporters," she said with confidence. She marched out and told the few remaining news people that they were going to church, and that if anyone thrust a microphone into the car, or asked her Jenny any questions, she would personally escort them to jail and wait there until they locked them up. **"Do I make myself clear?"**

One of the reporters stepped up and shoved a microphone in Argo's face. "What do you...?"

Argo brushed the microphone away and moved in close to the reporter, nose to nose. **"Do I make myself clear?"**

Argo and the reporter stared at each other for a moment before the reporter lowered his eyes and backed down. He retreated, rejoining the other news people. Argo sniffed and glared at the whole group before turning on her heels and marching back into the house.

Jenny giggled. Argo didn't let anyone intimidate her. She could handle any situation. When Argo marched back into the house, Jenny threw her arms around her, even if they could only fit halfway. "You were wonderful, Argo!"

Argo smiled. "I just couldn't let them bother you anymore, Jenny. Now, let's get ready for church."

The ride to church was uneventful, but people turned and stared at Jenny as she walked through the door. Mandy was sitting close to the door, so Jenny slid in beside her. All this attention was beginning to bother her.

"We'll be right across the aisle," Mr. Jenkins leaned down and whispered.

Jenny nodded.

Mandy whispered, "Reporters followed our car all the way to church. My dad had to yell at them to get away so I could get out of the car."

"Argo yelled at them at our house," Jenny whispered back. "They didn't dare follow us."

Mandy giggled. "I wonder how Molly is."

"Me, too. Come on over this afternoon and we'll call her," Jenny said. She turned and saw Calvin come in the door. She motioned for him to join them.

"Isn't this cool?" he said as he joined the girls.

"It's getting annoying," Jenny whispered. "Those reporters are everywhere."

"I saw Argo yell at them this morning," Calvin whispered with a smile.

"Yeah," Jenny smiled back. She turned her attention to the front of the church. The choir was coming in from the side doors and the chimes were ringing to signal that the church service was about to start.

During the service the minister said a prayer of thanks for the children who had rescued Molly and had averted a terrible situation. Jenny, Mandy, and Calvin smiled. Several people congratulated the children after the service was over. Jenny and Mandy seemed embarrassed, but Calvin smiled and enjoyed every comment.

That afternoon, Mandy skipped over to Jenny's house. Together they called Molly. Molly cried when she heard their voices. "I was so scared until you guys came," she sobbed. "Thank you so much."

Jenny and Mandy cried on the other end of the phone. They were glad that they had helped save her.

"My dad thinks that all of you should get a reward."

"We don't need a reward," Jenny answered. "We're just glad you're safe."

A loud knock sounded on Jenny's front door. "Jenny! Jenny!" Calvin's voice yelled.

Jenny ran to the door, still holding the cordless phone. "Come on in, Calvin. What's up?"

"You're never going to believe this!" Calvin exclaimed.

"What?" Jenny demanded.

"Kathy Jackson escaped from jail!"

"Who's Kathy Jackson?"

"The woman kidnapper!" Calvin said breathlessly.

Chapter Twelve

Mr. Jenkins jumped up from his chair in the living room, the Sunday paper dropping to the floor. "Close the door, Calvin." He looked at Jenny. "You kids stay away from the windows."

Molly overheard the conversation. She sobbed into the phone, "Jenny, I'm really scared. She's a mean lady."

"You need to tell your dad about this, Molly," Jenny advised. "Don't go outside."

"Don't worry, I won't," Molly sobbed.

"I'll call the rest of the girls and tell them," Jenny said. "There's no telling whose house she'll go to. We were all on the news."

"She knows where I live," Molly sobbed.

"Tell your dad. He can call the police and get you protection or something. That's what they do on TV."

"Okay," Molly said. "Call me later."

"Will do," Jenny said. "Bye."

"Bye," Molly answered.

"Mandy and Calvin can stay here for now," Argo said. "They'll be safe here."

Calvin giggled. "I saw how you ran off that reporter this morning. They still haven't come back."

"That woman better not come here," Argo said

with her hands on her hips. "She'll wish she hadn't if she does."

Mandy and Jenny giggled.

"I need to call the rest of the girls and warn them," Jenny said. She was still holding the phone, so she punched in Susan's number. Jenny told her to call Jackie, and she'd call Angie and Christy.

"You need to make your calls quick," Mr. Jenkins said. "I need to call Sergeant Anderson to see what we can do to protect you."

"Okey-dokey," Jenny answered. She punched in Angie's number.

Marylou peeked out the window. "There's a green truck going slow out there."

Argo looked out. "That's Mr. Johnson's truck."

"Who's Mr. Johnson?" Marylou asked.

"He's the old man who sells corn and tomatoes at the Farmer's Market."

"But Mr. Johnson wasn't driving it," Marylou said. "Someone with long dark hair was."

"Kathy Jackson has long dark hair," Mandy said.

"Tell Angie to call Christy," Mr. Jenkins said to Jenny. "I need to use the phone, now."

Jenny quickly got off the phone and handed it to her father, who punched in 9-1-1. He told the dispatcher about the truck and asked her to also check on Mr. Johnson at his farm. "I believe the escaped kidnapper may have stolen his truck. Mr. Johnson may be hurt." When he put the phone back in its cradle, he turned to Jenny and said, "Why don't you kids check out the attic. You can show your friends some of our treasures up there."

Jenny laughed. "It's just a lot of old stuff. I never saw any treasure."

"Jenny's attic is cool," Calvin told Mandy. "We even saw squirrels up there once."

"Squirrels?" Mandy asked.

"Yeah. A mother squirrel and her babies," Calvin answered.

"You kids run along and play up there," Argo said. "You'll be safe up there. I'll call Mandy's dad and Calvin's mom to tell them that you'll be here awhile."

Jenny led the way up the stairs to the attic. The door creaked when she opened it. She flipped on the light to reveal boxes, pictures, old furniture, trunks, toys, and the usual array of stuff that gets put into an attic when the owners don't have a use for it anymore.

"Let's get out your Uncle Paul's military school uniform," Calvin suggested. He ran for the trunk where it was stored.

Mandy pointed to a covered porcelain bowl with flowers painted on it. "What's that?"

"That's a chamber pot," Jenny said. "Back in the old days, before people had indoor bathrooms, the chamber pot was put under the bed for people to use, so they wouldn't have to go outside in the dark to the outhouse."

"Ewww! Gross!" Mandy said with her nose crinkled up.

"Look," Calvin said. He was dressed up in a military coat and hat. He pretended he had a sword and was swinging his arm like he was fighting someone. Mandy and Jenny laughed.

The children played in the attic for almost an hour. They examined the pictures, the contents of the trunks and boxes, Jenny and Marylou's old toys, and tried on old-fashioned clothes. There was a big mirror stored over in the corner so they could admire themselves in each outfit.

The children heard a squeal of tires outside. Mr. Johnson's green truck stopped in front of Calvin's house. Calvin and Jenny peeked out the attic window, but they couldn't see who was in the truck. The barrel of a shotgun slowly stuck out the window and pointed at Calvin's house. A shot rang out. Mandy screamed. Jenny put her hand over Mandy's mouth.

"She's shooting at my house!" Calvin exclaimed.

Another shot rang out. The truck peeled away from the curb and sped down the street.

The children ran down the stairs. "Did you see that?" Jenny asked.

"I heard gunfire, but I didn't see anything," Argo said. She had closed all the curtains and blinds downstairs, so no one could see in or out.

"Someone just shot at my house!" Calvin yelled. "I've got to go and see if my mom's all right!"

"You kids stay here," Mr. Jenkins said. "I'll go and check on your mom. Argo, please call Sergeant Anderson and tell him what just happened here." He went out the back door and cut across the yard to Calvin's back porch. He called to Mrs. Kelly as he ran up the stairs so she'd know who was there. She wasn't hurt, just shaken up from the shooting. Mr. Jenkins put his arm around her, leading her out the door, and over to his house. He knew she shouldn't stay alone.

"Someone shot out one of my front windows," she told Argo when she stepped into the kitchen. Argo had just hung up the phone. Sergeant Anderson wasn't in the precinct, so she had told the desk sergeant who had answered the phone. He promised to send someone out to check on them and warned her not to go outside.

Mr. Jenkins noticed that Calvin's mom was shaking. "You can stay here until it's safe to go home," Mr. Jenkins said. "That goes for you, too, Mandy."

"Thanks. I need to call my dad." Permission was granted. Argo went into the kitchen to cook. She hummed the whole time she was preparing the meal. She loved to cook, and cooking took her mind off the stressful matters at hand. Calvin's mom peeled the potatoes while Jenny and Marylou set the table. It would be like a party if it weren't such a scary time. The children were warned to stay away from the windows and doors. Two policemen knocked on the door and asked if they were all right, then promised to patrol the immediate neighborhood to see if they could spot the shooter. Mr. Jenkins called Mandy's dad to invite him to join them for dinner. The dining room table was pulled to the side of the room out of the line of fire, if someone should shoot through the windows.

After a platterful of pork chops, a mountain of mashed potatoes, and a big bowl of corn had been devoured, Argo brought out a chocolate cake she had made that afternoon. Just as she put the knife into it to cut the first piece, the lights went out. The room became too dark to see anything until the group's eyes adjusted to the light.

"I'm scared!" Mandy sobbed.

"Stay down and away from the windows," Mr. Jenkins ordered. "I'll call 9-1-1." He picked up the phone. It was dead. No dial tone. "The phone doesn't work."

"She must have cut the power and the phone line," Argo said. She was certain that the person who did this was Kathy Jackson.

"Not without being electrocuted," Mr. Jenkins said. "Unless…"

"Unless what?" Argo asked.

"Unless she knew how to turn off the power at the meter outside or unless she turned off our circuit breaker," Mr. Jenkins said thoughtfully.

Argo's eyes widened. "But that's in the basement." She put her hand on her mouth, suddenly understanding. "She could be in the house!"

"I've got my cell phone," Mandy's dad said. He took the phone off his belt and punched in 9-1-1. After talking with the dispatcher, he folded the phone shut. "The police will be here within two minutes."

"I'll get candles," Marylou offered.

"No!" Mr. Jenkins told her. "Kathy Jackson doesn't know her way around our house. We do. We have the advantage."

Jenny jumped when a loud THUNK sounded on the basement stairs. "She's coming up," she whispered. She hugged Mandy.

Marylou sobbed quietly.

"Take cover behind anything you can," Mr. Jenkins said. "We know she's armed."

Mandy, Calvin, and Jenny hid behind the sofa. Marylou ducked behind the computer table. Calvin's mom and Argo tiptoed to the front hall closet, slipped in, and left the door open just a crack. Mandy's dad and Mr. Jenkins stood on each side of the kitchen door, hoping to grab Kathy Jackson when she came through.

Mr. Jenkins heard it first. A creak of the basement door as it opened.

"She's coming in the kitchen," he whispered. He grabbed a heavy vase of flowers off the table beside the door and held it up over his head. The door to the kitchen swung open, and Mr. Jenkins hit someone square on top of the head. The person fell forward, landing on the carpet at his feet. Mr. Jenkins lit a match to see who it was.

"This isn't Kathy Jackson!" he exclaimed. "It's a man!"

Chapter Thirteen

"**W**ho is it?" Argo asked from the crack in the closet door.

"A man with long dark hair," Mr. Jenkins replied.

"I thought it was that woman," Jenny said as she stood up from behind the sofa. "She has long dark hair."

A loud knock sounded at the front door, a distinct

three-rap knock. A loud voice called, **"Police."** Argo slipped out of the closet and opened the door to reveal the same two uniformed policemen standing on the porch who had come earlier. Marylou went into the kitchen to light some emergency candles Argo kept in the cupboard under the sink. She set one in the living room and one on the dining room table.

"What's the problem here?" the tall policeman asked.

"A man broke into the house and cut off our power and phone lines," Argo explained.

"Where is he?" the same policeman asked.

"He's over here, officer," Mr. Jenkins replied. "I knocked him out with a vase of flowers." Mr. Jenkins pointed to the floor.

The policeman took his heavy duty flashlight from his belt and turned it on. He shined it on the man lying on the floor. "That's Ken Jackson. "We've had trouble with him before." He took handcuffs from the back of his belt, pulled Ken Jackson's hands around his back, and cuffed him.

"Ken Jackson?" Jenny asked. "Does he have a sister named Kathy?"

"As a matter of fact he does. She's bad news, too."

"She was one of Molly's kidnappers," Calvin said. "She escaped from jail this afternoon. We thought it was her in the truck shooting at my house."

"All we saw was the long dark hair," Mandy told the policeman. "We thought it was that nasty woman."

A soft moan escaped from Ken Jackson.

"He's coming around," the policeman said. "It's best we get him out of here. We can question him down at the precinct."

"Wait!" Mr. Jenkins said. "We still might be in danger. Where's Kathy Jackson?"

"Maybe she's at her brother's house," Calvin suggested. "Maybe her brother is trying to help her."

"Or she could be here, too," Jenny whispered with her eyes wide. "Maybe she's in the basement."

"I'll call for back-up to search the premises," the officer promised. He spoke into a small device clipped to his shoulder and called the station. The other officer put Ken Jackson into the back seat of the patrol car, carefully pushing his head down so he wouldn't bump it, and locked the door.

Sirens pierced the night air. A patrol car squealed to a stop behind the first car. Another raced to the scene. Four policemen jumped out of the cars. Sergeant Anderson drove up with two more uniformed officers.

A news truck from Channel Five rushed to the scene and stopped abruptly in front of Calvin's house.

"You need to come out of the house while we look for the fugitive," Sergeant Anderson told Mr. Jenkins. "How many more are in the house?"

Since everyone had come out on the porch to watch the policeman put Ken Jackson into the police car, Mr. Jenkins replied, "I think we're all here."

"Good. Is there somewhere you can go, other than your front porch?"

"We could go to my house," Mandy's dad offered.

"Where is that?" Sergeant Anderson asked.

"Over there, just across the street," he answered, pointing to his red brick ranch-style house.

Sirens pierced the night once more. A SWAT team truck squealed to a stop in the middle of the street. Several SWAT team members jumped out. Sergeant Anderson went to talk to them.

Two SWAT team members asked for the house keys from Mandy's dad, so they could check out the house before the families went in. That done, Jenny's, Mandy's, and Calvin's families paraded across the street with two police officers to protect them. No one noticed the camera from the news van recorded every move they made and scanned the house to which they were heading.

Once in, one of the officers locked the door, the other checked all the other doors. The house seemed secure, but the officers told the families to stay together in the living and dining rooms and not to go anywhere by themselves, even to the bathroom.

Across the street at the Jenkins' home, the SWAT team entered, their guns drawn in one hand and a large flashlight in the other. After a short time, all the officers came out of the house, replaced their guns in their holsters, and put their flashlights back in their belts.

Sergeant Anderson walked across the street and knocked three times, hard, on the door. "The main circuit breaker was cut off, so we flipped it on again. We didn't find anyone in your house, but that doesn't mean you have to ease up on your guard. Kathy Jackson is still at large and is still a menace to you. She could show up at any time. He looked at Mrs. Kelly and asked, "Is there any place you and Calvin could go? Do you have any relatives nearby?"

Argo stepped up to Sergeant Anderson. "They can stay with us until all this blows over. The girls can bunk together, and Mrs. Kelly and Calvin can use the other bedroom."

Calvin and Jenny smiled at each other. They both were thinking that this could be fun.

Argo caught the look between them. She put her hands on her hips and said, "This is not going to be fun and games. This is serious business. Kathy Jackson may be out to get you."

The two friends sobered up.

Argo continued, "And furthermore, there will be no going downstairs at night by yourselves, at least not until Kathy Jackson is caught."

"Argo's right," Mr. Jenkins said. "Stay with someone at all times. If you have to get up during the night, for any reason, let someone know where you're going."

"Mrs. Kelly," one of the uniformed officers said, "I'll walk you to your house and stay with you while you get the things you and Calvin need to spend the night and dress for tomorrow."

"Mr. Jenkins, I'll have an unmarked patrol car on the street in front of your house with two officers for your protection 24/7 until this matter gets resolved," Sergeant Anderson told him.

"What about school?" Jenny asked. She couldn't wait to get back to school to tell everyone about what happened.

"I'm afraid that going to school tomorrow would be too risky for any of you children, especially those involved in the kidnapping/rescue yesterday. We'll have officers contact the other parents as well," Sergeant Anderson said in a very authoritive voice.

Marylou, Jenny, and Calvin looked crushed. They all wanted to go to school. After all, excitement like this had just never happened on this street before. Everyone at school would be talking about it, and they wanted to be in on it, too.

Chapter Fourteen

Jenny heard the noise first. It was a small creak, like someone was coming up the stairs. She poked Marylou and whispered, "Someone's on the steps." Marylou was instantly awake, eyes wide and frightened.

Jenny jumped up quickly and tiptoed through Marylou's room to her room where Calvin and his mom were sleeping. She tiptoed to Calvin's side of the bed, shook him gently, and whispered about the noise on the stairs. Calvin was instantly awake. He sat up quickly, waking his mother. While Calvin was whispering to his mother, Jenny ran to her closet and pulled out her baseball bat for herself and a cap gun, which she handed to Calvin.

Marylou stumbled out of her bedroom and hid behind the door in Jenny's room, too scared to be left alone, but not brave enough to help Jenny.

Another creak, this time closer. Everyone froze and listened. Cre-e-ak! Whoever was coming up the stairs was almost there.

Jenny recognized the step that made the creak. She motioned for Calvin to come. They tiptoed to the top of the stairs and peeked around the corner. The light from the aquarium at the bottom of the stairs made it possible for Jenny and Calvin to see a shadow coming toward them, but whoever was on the stairs only saw darkness ahead so the children couldn't be seen.

When the creeper reached the top step, Jenny held the bat over her head, and Calvin pulled the trigger on the cap gun. The loud noise startled the creeper, and whoever it was turned and half ran and half stumbled down the stairs.

Jenny lowered the bat and let out a huge sigh.

By that time everyone in the house was awake. Lights snapped on, feet hit the floor, and Mr. Jenkins yelled, "What's going on?" Downstairs, the front screen door slammed against the frame with a loud bang.

"Who's shooting?" Argo asked.

"I was," Calvin said proudly. "Someone was tiptoeing up the stairs, and we scared him away with a cap gun!"

"Who's we?" Argo asked.

"Us," Calvin and Jenny said together, holding up their weapons.

"Why didn't you wake me?" Mr. Jenkins asked.

"There wasn't time," Jenny explained. "By the time I would have gone all the way down to your room, whoever was on the steps would have been up here."

"Young lady, whoever it was is probably very dangerous, and probably had a real gun," Mr. Jenkins replied.

"But," Calvin argued, "he probably would have shot someone, if he had been able to get to any one of us."

"That is true," Argo answered. "I believe that Jenny and Calvin were very brave and may have saved one or all of our lives tonight." She smiled broadly at the children, with her hand on her chest. "I, for one, am eternally grateful."

Jenny and Calvin smiled back.

At that moment a policeman appeared at the open front door. "Are you folks all right? We saw someone run out of the door. My partner is chasing him, but I came to check on you."

"We're fine, thanks to Jenny and Calvin. They

scared whoever it was out of here," Mr. Jenkins said from the top of the steps.

"We need to talk," the policeman said. "Will you all please come downstairs?"

Everyone dashed back into their bedrooms to gather up slippers and robes. Once covered, they walked downstairs to two waiting policemen. "I'm sorry, but I lost who I was chasing," the policeman with O'Neal on his nametag said. "I called my captain, and he's on the way over here. I don't need to tell you that you are in grave danger until Kathy Jackson is caught." He looked sternly from face to face as he talked. "We'll have officers searching the neighborhood, but there are too many places to hide in the dark. If we don't find anyone, we will leave an officer in the house for the remainder of the night. Then, I would suggest that you relocate for a few days."

"Relocate!" Argo exclaimed. "Where? We can't move in on friends or family. They'd be put in danger."

At that moment, Captain Mixon walked in. He

introduced himself then said, "We probably need to relocate tonight. It's too dangerous for you to stay here with Kathy Jackson on the loose. We'll put you in a safe house or a guarded hotel room. We wouldn't want anyone else to be in danger."

"How long would we have to be there?" Mr. Jenkins asked. "We have work and school."

"I understand," the captain replied. "But, the important thing now is to keep you safe. Now go pack enough for three days."

"Three days!" Marylou, Jenny, and Calvin shouted together.

"You probably won't need that much, but it's better to have too much than too little. Also, I need your work and school phone numbers. We will call them and explain the situation. If you call, someone could trace it. Do not use your cell phones or the internet. They could be traced."

"No cell phones! No email!" Marylou cried. "I will die!"

Jenny laughed. "No you won't. It isn't that important. Just think, in the olden days when Dad and Argo were kids, there weren't any cell phones or internet."

Argo interrupted by saying, "Quickly, girls, go pack. We need to leave right away."

Jenny and Marylou followed Argo upstairs, and Calvin and his mother went next door, escorted by two policemen. Mr. Jenkins talked to Captain Mixon for a few moments before he went upstairs to pack.

Argo and the girls were almost packed when Officer O'Neal called upstairs for everyone to come back downstairs. Mrs. Kelly and Calvin walked in the door, and Officer O'Neal asked them if they would please have a seat in the living room, for he needed to talk to everyone at once.

"What's up?" Jenny asked. She ran over and sat on the floor beside Calvin.

When everyone was seated, Officer O'Neal told the two families that two of their officers had just caught Kathy Jackson speeding down Custer Avenue. "The officers seemed to think that she was high on drugs. They took her to the hospital to check that out. Meanwhile, it looks like you'll be safe here for tonight. I'll spend the rest of the night right here in the living room and patrol the downstairs. Two other patrolmen will be stationed outside."

Jenny and Calvin looked disappointed, but everyone else was relieved.

The two families, again, went upstairs to try to get some sleep.

Chapter Fifteen

Early Monday morning Jenny hopped out of bed. She smelled bacon cooking and was instantly reminded of Kathy Jackson in the old farmhouse. She tiptoed to her room where Calvin and Mrs. Kelly were sleeping. Mrs. Kelly was already up, but Calvin was still asleep. Not wanting to wake him, since they couldn't go to school anyway, she ran barefoot down the stairs.

Officer O'Neal was sitting at the kitchen table drinking a large mug of coffee. Argo and Mrs.

Kelly were preparing a breakfast of eggs, bacon, hash browns and toast. Argo hummed softly one of her old songs as she stirred the scrambled eggs. She loved to cook, and it took her mind off the dangers the household faced.

"Hi, everybody," Jenny called brightly. "When's breakfast?"

"Good morning, Jenny," Argo replied. "Breakfast is as soon as everyone gets down here. Why don't you go wake up Marylou and Calvin?"

"Where's Dad?"

"He left for work a little while ago," Argo answered. "He has to take care of some quick business, and he'll be right back. He said he doesn't want to be gone too long because of all that's happening around here."

"I'll wake everyone up," Jenny announced. She turned and ran back up the stairs calling, "Breakfast! Everyone get up!"

Marylou propped up on one elbow and rubbed her eyes with the other hand.

Calvin jumped out of bed and said, "All right!"

"Last one downstairs is a rotten egg!" Jenny called as she spun around and ran for the stairs. Calvin was right behind her. Marylou struggled out of bed and followed slowly.

"Jenny and Calvin, wash your hands and set the table," Argo instructed.

The two children ran for the small bathroom next to the kitchen and tried to get through the door at the same time. Officer O'Neal laughed.

Argo and Mrs. Kelly put the food on platters and set them in the middle of the table. Marylou walked into the kitchen right by the back door. The door flew open, and before anyone could react, someone grabbed Marylou around the neck and pointed a gun into the kitchen.

"Move, and this girl gets hurt!" the newcomer

yelled. "You messed with my kids, now I'll mess with yours!"

Jenny and Calvin, still in the bathroom, peeked out through the crack of the not quite closed door. Jenny shuddered. She looked wildly around the little room for something to use to protect them. She quietly opened the cabinet door and found a disinfectant spray can. She picked it up and held it behind her back. The newcomer had his back to the bathroom door and didn't see Jenny or Calvin.

"Put your gun on the floor and kick it over to me," the man instructed Officer O'Neal. "Try anything cute, and this girl gets it."

Marylou was so frightened that her face had gone completely white. She looked as if she were going to faint. Her eyes began to roll back in her head, and then she went limp.

Officer O'Neal did as he was told, so he wouldn't endanger Marylou to a greater extent. Just as he kicked the gun, Marylou fell to the floor with a thunk.

Jenny peeked out of the bathroom, saw her chance, jumped out, and sprayed the man in the face with the disinfectant spray. His gun went off. The bullet hit the leg of the table, breaking it. The kitchen table fell down on one corner. Bacon, eggs, and hash browns slid off the platters onto the floor. Officer O'Neal grabbed for his gun, which was now covered with scrambled eggs. The man clawed at his eyes with his free hand, screaming that he was blind. He backed up and stumbled through the open back door pushing at the screen door.

Mrs. Kelly stood there as if in shock.

Argo looked at the ruined food in dismay.

Calvin yelled, "All right! You got him!"

Everything happened so fast.

Marylou opened her eyes. "What happened?" She felt her hair, which was now covered in hash browns. "Gross! What *is this?"*

Officer O'Neal was up and running out the door. He had scrambled eggs and bacon on his uniform.

He had slipped once in the food and almost fell on Marylou, but he caught the doorknob just in time.

Jenny and Calvin started to run after him, but Argo caught each of them by the arm and said, "Oh, no, you two don't. There might be shooting out there. Get down, away from the windows and door. Marylou, stay where you are!"

Everyone in the kitchen ducked down. Jenny's heart beat wildly. Calvin wiggled with excitement. Marylou put her hand over her eyes and moaned.

Someone thumped up the back porch steps. Argo jumped up with the frying pan clutched in both hands, ready to swing. She expected to see the man burst through the door with his gun. Instead, Officer O'Neal rapped quietly and let himself in. "I lost him," he admitted. "I went right out after him, but he was gone, like he vanished into thin air. I did see an old battered, black truck parked next door. I called in the license plate number. Maybe something will come of that."

"Did you look under the porch?" Jenny asked.

"I hide there sometimes when Calvin and I play hide and seek."

"To tell you the truth Jenny, I didn't," Officer O'Neal admitted. "I concentrated on him running as far and as fast as he could."

"But, he couldn't see very well," Argo pointed out. "He might have had to take the time for the disinfectant to clear out of his eyes a little."

Officer O'Neal rushed out of the house and thundered down the porch steps. He crawled under the porch and looked around with his flashlight. He saw something black and shiny near the end of the porch by the garage. He squirmed over and picked it up. It was a black shoe, still warm from being worn. Officer O'Neal crawled out of the opening and stood up. Just then, the black truck roared to life and took off down the street. He slowly walked back to the screen door, carrying the shoe.

"He was there, all right," Officer O'Neal admitted as he walked into the house. "Apparently, he was driving the old black truck, because it just took off." He turned to go back outside, muttering something about checking on the truck.

"At least we're safe for a while," Argo sighed. "Stand up everyone. Let's get this mess cleaned up and cook something else for us to eat."

Jenny heard her dad's truck in the driveway. "Dad's home!" she shouted. She started for the door, but Argo grabbed her just as she put her hand on the handle.

"Don't go out there just yet, Jenny. That man may still be close."

The truck door slammed, and Mr. Jenkins ran for the back door. "I just saw Officer O'Neal. He's a mess. What happened here?" he asked as he raced inside.

Argo filled him in on what just happened. Mr. Jenkins sat down hard on a kitchen chair. "You all could have been killed," he said. His voice trembled.

"But we weren't," Argo answered. "Your daughter is very brave in the face of danger. Without her quick thinking, things could have been much worse. She's a hero!"

Jenny smiled, happy that Argo appreciated her. She, however, didn't feel like a hero. Molly was the hero for not falling apart when she was kidnapped.

The phone rang suddenly, causing everyone to jump. Mr. Jenkins grabbed the receiver and said, "Hello." He listened for a few seconds and then handed the phone to Jenny. "It's for you. It's Angie."

Jenny took the phone. "Hi, Angie. What's up?" She listened for a minute or so. Her eyes grew wide. "Duck down and don't go near the windows or doors. I'll explain later. I'll call 9-1-1 and then call you back." She clicked off the phone and then punched in 9-1-1. She explained to the dispatcher who she was and what had happened. "Yes, I'll stay on the line," she stated. Jenny covered the mouthpiece with her hand and told everyone in the kitchen that the black truck was slowly going back and forth in front of Angie's house and that Angie was really, really scared.

Officer O'Neal thundered up the back steps. "I

just heard about the call. I'll call the station and have guards at each of the girl's houses within minutes. They will explain to each of the families why they are there." He turned and ran back to the police car.

A police siren was heard in the distance, then another and another, and another. Since all the girls lived fairly close to each other, all the sirens could be heard. One pulled up in front of Mandy's house, and a policeman jumped out. He ran to the door and rapped hard three times before Mandy's dad peeked out the front window.

Mr. Jenkins took the phone from Jenny and told her that he would wait on the line for her. After a couple of minutes, he said, "Thank you. I just want her to be safe." He hung up the phone and told Jenny that a policeman was at Angie's house, guarding her and her grandmother.

The phone rang. This time no one jumped. It was Molly. She wanted to know if Jenny and Calvin were all right. She had just called Angie and Jackie and was about to call the rest of the girls. Jenny told her what was happening. Molly started to cry. "It's because of me. I'm so sorry. If I hadn't gone near that van, none of this would have happened."

"It's not your fault, Molly," Jenny reassured her. "It could have happened to anyone. Besides, the only ones that are hurt are the kidnappers."

"That's true," Molly answered. "You, the girls, and Calvin were pretty awesome out at the farmhouse. I really didn't know anyone so brave before this. I don't think I could have done what all of you did."

"Sure you could, if you had to," Jenny told her.

"That woman, that Kathy Jackson, was so mean," Molly sobbed. "I think she would have killed me as well as her partners, if she had the chance. Thanks to you and the others in the club, she didn't get that chance."

"Call the others and let them know what's going on," Jenny interrupted. She didn't want Molly to be so sad. "I'll let you know of anything more happens here. Maybe the police will catch that man today, and we can all go back to school tomorrow. I feel funny about staying out today when I'm not sick."

"Me, too," Molly answered. "When everyone is caught, my dad wants to have a big party with the whole club and Calvin as honorees."

"Cool," Jenny said, "but let's not plan anything yet. We may have to wait awhile."

"Let's hope not," Molly answered. She didn't have the sadness in her voice that she did when she first started to talk to Jenny. "Call me later. Thanks for being there for me. Thanks for being my friend."

"You're welcome," Jenny smiled. "See you later." She hung up the phone.

Officer O'Neal rapped on the back door. "The man in the black truck was caught driving in front of Susan's house. It was Keith Jackson, father of Kathy and Ken. He admitted that he had helped Kathy escape from jail and that he was going to make someone pay for his kids getting arrested."

Argo uttered a sigh of relief. She held a dish towel against her chest and smiled.

"I'm afraid that Argo and you, Mr. Jenkins, will

now have to go to court and testify, also, because he broke into your house. You two probably will have to identify him."

"That won't be a problem, Officer, we both will be glad to do it," Mr. Jenkins said as he looked over at Argo.

Argo nodded and smiled. "I'd do anything to put him behind bars."

Chapter Sixteen

The weeks fairly flew by. Everyone in the Lost Mothers' Club was busy with school, identifying the kidnappers, talking to reporters, and being interviewed every time they were any place. It was a chore to even go out to play. They had been on the news for a week after the kidnapping. People were still asking for their autographs.

"It's not as much fun being famous as I thought it would be," Jenny complained to Mandy and Calvin one afternoon in Calvin's tree house.

Ann Westmoreland

"I know what you mean," Mandy answered. "My life's not like it was before."

"Did you know that no one can drive around Summerville in an ice cream truck and sell ice cream to kids anymore," Calvin told Jenny and Mandy.

"Really!" the girls chorused.

"Really," Calvin answered. "My mom found out about it from Officer O'Neal."

"I saw him grilling in your backyard last night," Jenny laughed. "What's going on?"

"They're dating," Calvin answered with a smile.

"Dating!" Jenny and Mandy shouted together

"They started dating the week after they caught the kidnappers."

"Why didn't you tell us?" Jenny asked.

"I didn't even know. I was at my dad's house when they went out. My mom didn't want to say

152

anything until she was sure she would like him. She just told me last night."

"That's awesome!" Jenny exclaimed. "I like him."

"Me, too," Mandy chimed in.

"I can't wait to tell Molly," Jenny smiled. "She feels so bad about what all has happened. She feels everything was her fault."

"Officer O'Neal asked me to call him Ben," Calvin told them. "But that's only when he's off duty."

"Maybe something good will come out of all this mess," Mandy said.

"Maybe," Jenny answered. She was thinking about calling Molly when she went in and telling her the news.

"It's been fun riding in a limousine to school and back," Mandy said. "Molly's dad said he would make sure we didn't have to walk alone for the rest of the school year."

"Did you know that the driver is a bodyguard?" Calvin asked. "I saw his gun when his suit jacket flew open that last windy day. I asked Molly about it, and she said it was true."

"Really?" Mandy answered. "I guess Molly's dad wants to be sure we're safe."

Mandy, Jenny, and Calvin climbed down the ladder Jenny and Calvin had made together last year by nailing boards to the tree. Their parents and Marylou were afraid to climb it so anything they talked about in the tree house was only between them and their friends. Pete even slept in it one night when his stepmother was mad at him and chased him out of the house. He was so frightened of her that he climbed into the tree house and stayed there, knowing she wouldn't find him there.

Jenny went home and called Molly who was bubbling with excitement. "Guess what!" she almost shouted into the phone.

"What?" Jenny laughed. She hadn't heard her friend so happy since before her mom left.

"My dad has a surprise for the whole club!"

"What is it?" Jenny asked, very interested.

"I promised I wouldn't tell until everyone could hear it at once."

"When will that be?"

"Tomorrow night. Everyone in the club and their parents are invited over for a cookout in our backyard."

"Is Argo invited, too?"

"Sure."

Jenny was so excited she could hardly stand still. "You can't give me just a little hint?"

"No, I promised."

"Well, okay." Jenny did understand. "Oh, I almost forgot why I called in the first place. I have some news, too. Calvin's mom is dating Officer O'Neal."

"No way!" Molly squealed.

"Yes, way. Not only that, but Officer O'Neal asked Calvin to call him Ben when he wasn't on duty."

"What does Calvin think about all that?"

"He seems happy. He misses his dad, so maybe this will help." Jenny was smiling. She was happy for Calvin.

"I'll tell Argo and Dad about tomorrow," Jenny said. "I'll see you at school in the morning. Thanks."

"You're welcome. But, it's me who should be thanking you. All of you saved my life."

"You're our friend," Jenny answered. "We couldn't let anything happen to you."

"I'm so glad I have friends like you."

"See you later," Jenny said. She was anxious to tell Argo and her dad about tomorrow.

* * * * * * *

The next evening all the families of the Lost

Mothers' Club gathered in Molly's backyard. The butler had greeted them and ushered them through the living room and the library and through French double doors to the backyard. Musicians played softly in the corner of the patio. White tablecloths hung to the ground covering round tables decorated with fresh flowers, and long tables held enormous amounts of food. Lights seem to hang everywhere.

"Oh, my!" Argo exclaimed with her hand on her chest. "I feel like royalty."

Molly's dad came up behind her and said, "You should feel that way. You have helped raise a wonderful and very brave girl."

"This is not like any cookout I've ever been to before," Mandy's dad whispered to Mandy. He was watching the chefs prepare their creations on long grills.

"This is wonderful," Mrs. Kelly confided to Officer O'Neal, who was invited to escort Calvin and his mom.

After eating huge platefuls of food, topped off

with make your own sundaes for the children and exotic desserts for the adults, Mandy's dad tapped his water glass with his spoon and said, "You all must be wondering why I invited you here tonight. Well, I am so very grateful to the brave children here who did what the police could not. They found my daughter. No offense to you, Officer O'Neal." Everyone laughed. "To get to the point, I want to do something special for all of you. Without you, Molly probably would not be here tonight."

Molly was smiling. The rest of the audience was wondering what he was going to say next.

Molly's dad continued, "As you probably have guessed, money is not one of the things I worry about, so I decided to do something for you."

Angie poked Susan and whispered, "I wonder what it is!"

Molly's dad continued, "After the kidnappers' trial, where I'm sure they'll be sentenced to a good long time behind bars, I've decided to take the club members and a parent to Disneyworld in Florida. We will travel together in my RV, which is as big as a bus, so we won't be crowded. We'll stay at The Polynesian Village. All expenses will be paid, so all you have to bring is you and some clothes."

Everyone stood up and clapped.

"We will be gone a week, so try to make some arrangements for the first week in July," Molly's dad shouted above the noise. He was smiling and enjoying their appreciation.

"I have another surprise for the club members that even Molly doesn't know about. I have set up a trust fund for all seven of you to use for college tuition. You will have four years paid for, providing you work hard and make passing grades. If you get into trouble with the law or fail your classes, the trust fund will be cut off. I believe that is fair."

Everyone stood up and clapped again.

The parents all went over to thank Molly's dad and the children got together to talk about the wonderful things that happened this evening. All in all, it was a very generous offer, and they all vowed to stay out of trouble and make good grades so they could get into college.

The rest of the school year went by quickly. The trial was over, and all the kidnappers and Mr. Jackson had been found guilty and sentenced to prison for a good long time. Every one of the club members and a parent boarded the RV bus and had a wonderful time in Orlando, Florida. They all promised to live up to the conditions that Mandy's dad had set for college. After all, something like this doesn't come along very often.